A Fated Night

A Novel

Cynthia Dane
BARACHOU PRESS

A Fated Night

Copyright: Cynthia Dane
Published: 25ʰ November 2016
Publisher: Barachou Press

This is a work of fiction. Any and all similarities to any characters, settings, or situations are purely coincidental.

All rights reserved. No part of this publication may be reproduced, stored in retrieval system, copied in any form or by any means, electronic, mechanical, photocopying, recording or otherwise transmitted without written permission from the publisher. You must not circulate this book in any format.

Chapter 1

"Perhaps You've Heard Of Her."

"A rabbit? Are you kidding? That's the best you could do?" Lana Losers almost dropped the sticker her boss Roger had given her at the last minute. "A fucking rabbit."

Roger snapped his spine straight, played with the one button he would ever fuss with on his jacket, and smirked at his protégé as if she owed him the world. At least he never bothered her for sex. *Too gay for that.* One of the many reasons she had decided to work for his agency over others that had offered her more money. "It matches your charm, Lana." He carefully placed the golden sticker of a rabbit on her nametag. Roger had already taken the liberty of writing LANA LOSERS on the hopping bunny. "Besides, it makes you stick out. You *want* to stick out here, babe. You're the fucking star of the conference."

She wouldn't argue with that, but Lana already couldn't get people to take her seriously in the real estate world. If someone wasn't trying to grab her ass on her way by their desk, they were asking her for coffee or for something more pornographic. That was at her firm! *HR doesn't give a shit. HR hits on me too.* Roger was the only one who wasn't always trying to get beneath her skirt. Instead, he called her *babe* and occasionally asked her to beard for him when they dealt with more conservative clients. *"I dream of a day when nobody cares that I'm gay, babe,"* he often said after too much wine. *"You'd think that in the year of our Lord, 2003, nobody would care, but…"*

Lana didn't care about his problems. She cared about *her* problems. Every time some man tried to bring her down, she worked twice as hard. Within two years of graduating from grad school, Lana Losers had become one of the most successful real estate agents in New England. *We're not talking bungalows and bodegas, either.* Lana had always had her sights on big ticket items. Skyscrapers. Mansions. Sure, she cut her teeth on old Victorian homes and office parks, but once she settled on the high-end commercial shit, she was making more money than she knew what to do with. As a woman who grew up in a house full of millionaires? That said a lot. *Those million-dollar connections got me my job, though.* She didn't spring for nepotism, but she did happily take her father's suggestion that he introduce her to some of his buddies from the country club.

Now here she was, at the tender age of twenty-seven, prepared to accept the award for most successful agent, 2002-2003.

A Fated Night

Roger was the first to tell her that she was getting too big for his firm in the DC metro area. Lana was meant for bigger and better things. However, even though he was willing to pawn her off to a big firm from Boston, Philadelphia, or even New York, he wanted that headhunter's fee. Millions and millions of dollars' worth of headhunting fees.

While she knew it was in her best interest, Lana still felt like a young bride and Roger was her father, sizing up suitors in the hopes that his dowry would pay off. Or maybe she was a bovine. A heifer. Damnit, Lana Losers was no heifer!

Roger already botched it by reporting the wrong name to the conference organizer. When they showed up and found a nametag that said *Linda Losario* waiting for them, Lana was halfway to livid. Roger popped into the nearest office supply store and came back with…

A golden rabbit nametag. So childish that Lana felt even worse than before.

She wanted these firms and agencies to take her seriously, damnit. There was no guarantee that she would once again be the best selling commercial agent next year. Now was her big chance to leave favorable impressions on the chairmen and CEOs of America's top real estate agencies. If she wanted them to entrust her with properties worth tens of millions of dollars? She had to look professional. That's why she wore a black skirt suit as opposed to her signature purple or red. She pulled her long blond hair back into a clean, conscious bun dotted with black lacquer pins. Her jewelry was expensive yet understated. Her heels gave her a commanding height over other women and the shorter men at the conference, but she was still able to walk with a confidant gait. She had even practiced her handshakes and her manner of speaking in front of a mirror. *Don't look too friendly. They'll think you're their mother or their girlfriend if you're too friendly.*

Lana Losers had taken her last name to heart growing up. While hardly anyone in her family was a *loser,* it did carry a certain negative connotation. *I'm a winner. I'm going to be the biggest winner this room has ever seen.* After a few deep breaths, she allowed Roger to lead her back into the main conference hall.

The meat of the conference started the next day and would last the next three. But the mixer that afternoon was one of the most crucial. Networking was the lifeblood of the real estate world, especially when it was a world full of friendly (and not-so-friendly) rivalries that could either make or break careers. Agents ditched their firms and ran off with other ones. Marriages were brokered as if they were properties. Women like Lana? Well, there were so few of them, let alone ones as conventionally attractive as her, that she turned enough heads to give her motion sickness.

Roger paraded her in front of his contemporaries and her potential new bosses. Here in the heart of New York City, it was easy to meet the men (it was always men) controlling some of the biggest firms in the nation. Some of them… were a little too eager to meet her. For all the wrong reasons.

"You are absolutely *radiant,*" said a manager of New York's second biggest firm. "Who does your makeup, love? My wife would kill to look like you!"

A Fated Night

Lana forced a smile as she allowed this uncouth gentleman to kiss her hand. For more than seconds. Ugh. "Oh, you know," she bullshitted, "I do my own makeup. Nothing special. Perhaps I'm a natural beauty."

The manager took a step back. *Too blunt for you? Too confident? Sorry, pal, no Demure Debbies over here.* Besides, she highly doubted that this man's wife wanted to look like her. More like he wanted his wife to do so. *He'll hit on me in 3… 2…*

"If you ever have the time, Ms. Losers, I'd love to discuss your future over some Chardonnay." Whomp. There it was.

A half hour passed in a blur trapped in molasses. *These men from all directions and taking my time. Feels like the worst gangbang ever.* Dear Lana had been in a couple, too. She would know.

"Make it stop," she finally said to Roger. She pressed her hand upon her stomach in an effort to settle the bile gurgling there. Not only did she need food, but she needed a hard drink. When was this mixer over? When could she go to the hotel bar and dump Roger for the night? Surely a bartender would be better conversation. Maybe he'd even be cute. Lana didn't care if her convention fucktoys only made minimum wage plus tips. If they could do her right, she'd take anyone to her room. "Or at least let my brain rest for ten minutes."

"Come on, Lana." Roger tugged on her arm as if he were a caveman. *Grab my hair while you're at it!* "One last man to introduce you to. I promise. Then you can go tinkle in the girl's room, if that's what you want."

At least Roger never expected smiles from his star pupil. He only expected commissions. Commissions out his *ass*.

"Ah, David!" Roger flagged down the last man he wanted to introduce Lana to. "Is that Andrews with you? Both of you come over here and shake my fucking hand! I've got the best person you're going to meet at this conference here with me!"

Lana barely paid attention as two men approached them. One was tall, the other considerably shorter. Both had dark hair and wore similar three-piece Brioni suits – except the taller man had a gold vest, and the shorter sported a royal purple sprinkled with forest green. Neither wore ties. They didn't have to. Their collars were slightly turned up and their cufflinks made out of pure gold. Lana knew who they worked for before the introductions began. *Lois & Bachman. The biggest firm in New York City.*

"Allow me to introduce you to Lana Losers. Perhaps you've heard of her? She's picking up the award for most sales in the past year." There was that hand clap again. Right on her shoulder, shaking her down to her core. *Bastard.* Like she was his son he could show off at the country club. Roger didn't even have a son!

"Pleasure," said the taller man.

"I've heard of her, yes," said the shorter.

"That's David Bachman, the third son of Mr. Bachman himself," Roger whispered in Lana's ear. "Not doing too badly for himself. The other is Ken Andrews, the #1 manager at the firm. So, you know, practically God of New York real estate."

Now that sort of info piqued Lana's interest. Nothing wrong with getting to know a man like that. Which one was it, though? It had to be the tall man in the gold vest. Tall men

A Fated Night

were more confident, more successful. Everyone knew that. Even Lana. *Especially* Lana. She had to deal with men's insecurities all day long.

The shorter man was the first to extend his hand. Lana had her eyes so intensely focused on the tall gentleman that she almost missed the handshake. "Oh!" she said, shedding the funk from her arms. "Sorry. Pleasure to meet you."

The man's firm handshake surprised her. Short. Quick. *Confident.* Arrogantly confidant. This was a man who had sold billions of dollars' worth of real estate in his time. "Ken Andrews," he unexpectedly said.

Well, there was a twist Lana was not expecting.

Ken Andrews did not look the typical real estate mogul, let alone the head manager of New York's #1 agency. *A man only makes it to that level if he's proved himself.* "Very nice to meet you, Mr. Andrews," Lana said. Her eyes remained locked on his, dark and powerful. Yet not so dark that they were sinister. Lots of underhanded pricks like that in the real estate world. No, something *glistened* in those wide eyes lined with only the slickest brows a man could boast. Ken was not the tallest man in the room, but he rivaled Lana even in her heels, and that was enough to allow a mutual attraction to occur. Plus, how could she look away from that goatee carefully groomed along his jaw and upper lip? *So trendy!* Lana liked her men in two flavors: hot and hairy, or young and bare. *Come on, girl, you didn't come here to flirt with these guys.* She had come here to change her life.

"You're surprised," Ken observed, standing back again. His stature never slumped or broadcasted anything but the greatest demeanor. *All right. I'm on board. This guy is successful.* "Don't give me that look, Ms. Losers. You know what it's like to buck trends in this industry. Also, I'm taller than Tom Cruise."

She laughed.

Why oh *why* did she laugh? Roger glanced at her. David Bachman looked greatly amused at the situation unfolding before him. Ken? His smile was so suave that Lana wondered if the room had heated up. *Yup. Furnace blasting between my legs. That's nice.* What the hell was wrong with her? She had only met this man for two seconds and was already wondering what it would be like to sit on his face?

Whoa. Lana needed to regroup. She also really needed that hard drink.

"You're quite the talk around here, Ms. Losers." Even the way Ken said her name was deliberately perfect. Not many got it right. They said it literally. *L-o-s-e-r.* With an S. So there was more than one loser in the room… which was always a riot when she and the rest of her family went out to functions that called for them to be formally heralded. So few realized that it was pronounced *Low-siers.* Even fewer realized her first name was pronounced Lay-na and not Lah-na. Apparently her parents did not care how their oldest child was introduced around the world. "We were shocked to see a newcomer do so well. It's not often the industry sees a ringer like you."

He didn't say that the most shocking thing was that she was a woman, but it was implied. *So much for that attraction.* Short men. Always passive-aggressive. Ken wouldn't say that she was an anomaly, but he would make sure she felt it in her bones.

A Fated Night

Or maybe somewhere else.

"If you two have time," Roger interrupted, "We would love to meet up for dinner sometime this week. There is a lot to discuss, I'm sure you know."

Ken turned his attention to him. Even though he had to look up to meet Roger's eyes, he did not falter. *My God. He's one of the most alpha men in this room.* Lana looked around. That said a lot. A lot! "Indeed. We'll see if we can cram a dinner into our schedule. I'm sure you understand that we're some of the most popular people here, whether to our benefit or not."

Roger laughed uneasily. Lana crossed her arms, drawing attention to her chest and the nametag upon it. Ken's attention.

"A bunny?" he mused out loud. "You have to be careful with those rabbits, Roger." He tipped the folder he carried toward the man he addressed. "You know what they say about them in the Chinese Zodiac. Very cunning. Very quick to rip off your balls." He gave Lana a furtive glance as he and David Bachman walked away. "Conflict avoidant."

Lana huffed. "I wasn't even born in the year of the rabbit. Wait. Was I?" She'd have to look it up.

Roger shook his head. "We're never going to get a dinner with them. Hope you liked any of the other firms here today, Lana. Because Ken Andrews does not seem to be trifled with us."

"What makes you think that?" Really? *Really?* After all that? After the burning in her stomach and the possible heartburn making its way up her esophagus? Over a man who was barely as tall as she was... in these heels?

"Because he fancies you, babe." Roger walked toward the men's room. "Ken Andrews doesn't piss his business where he fucks."

The mere insinuation was insulting! Yet Lana looked back to where Ken Andrews had gone, hoping to catch a glimpse of that confidant stature and gentle gaze. Unfortunately, most of the other men at the conference were either as tall as or taller than him, and he was lost in a haze of black business suits and the rabble of business mixed with pleasure.

Somehow, though… she felt him in that mob. His presence. His attitude. His no-nonsense way of parting a crowd so he could step through. Ken Andrews was somewhere in that mix, and he was not intimidated to be there. Lana could learn a lot from him.

A Fated Night

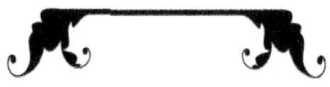

Chapter 2

"You Came To Flirt With Me, Mr. Andrews."

Ken had his pick of dinner associates. When a man was the head manager of New York's #1 real estate agency, he could have dinner with almost anyone in the city at a moment's notice.

He was used to a life of such privilege, however. As the second oldest son of the Andrews' investment fortune, Ken had been reared to grab life by the balls and squeeze them until money popped out. His father had taught all four Andrews boys to invest, invest, invest. He didn't care what his sons invested in. Technology. Women. *Stocks.* As long as their sons were investing – smartly – he could rest easy with the assumption that they could make their own names for themselves and not rely on their millions of dollars' worth of inheritance. So happened that the second oldest Andrews loved real estate and all it entailed. What better way to start investing than getting into rich, lucrative properties? Sitting, flipping, creating shell properties to boost other, underperforming ones... it was a very real game with even realer consequences. Good thing Ken took it seriously.

As seriously as he took women. Which was why he had forwent spending more than three minutes speaking with Lana Losers, the feminine star of that year's conference.

He had seen her photos in the magazines and newspapers before. Even online, although Ken tended to avoid the internet outside of checking his investments. Everyone who gave a shit about their business knew who Lana Losers was. Most knew her because she was riding a wave of success... *while* daring to be a gorgeous blond bombshell. *How dare she? Really.* She was quite a different specimen in real life, however. Although Ken had recognized her profile when he approached her and Roger Prescott, he hadn't anticipated the full effect of her face when it turned to him. That darling jawline, button nose, and pair of rosy cheeks... who had time to admire her judicious use of eyeliner and batting eyelashes when a face like that beckoned him? Ken had a weakness for beautiful women. A weakness he could keep in check, but weaknesses were weaknesses, nonetheless.

So he had to walk away as soon as it was socially acceptable to do so. For staying in Lana Losers' vicinity for much longer may have turned him into a slobbering idiot – and he was better than that.

A Fated Night

Besides, he was willing to bet that Lana had dealt with enough sexist bullshit to last her a few lifetimes. He didn't feel like adding to that because his cock got excited.

He and David had dinner with a west coast firm that had come out mostly for the networking. *Beverly Hills houses. Rodeo Drive studios. Nice, but nothing we do on a regular basis.* Lois & Bachman were so successful because they were niched to the point that nobody else could compete with them. When a man worked for the #1 go-to agency for selling skyscrapers (and not just the units within them,) it was a tough racket to beat.

Now Roger Prescott thinks I'm going to pay him to let me have Lana Losers on my team. He knew that's what Roger was after. How could he think of anything else while having dinner with Californian brokers who couldn't stop talking about the time difference? Ken could hardly pretend to care. He was going to return to his condo at the end of the evening, anyway. *Perks to living in New York, where everything happens.*

As soon as they shook the Californians, David suggested they wind down with a few cocktails at the hotel bar. A busy place, to be sure. Everyone coming in from out of town for the conference was staying in that hotel, and the bar was the most convenient place to get drinks, schmooze, and pretend that the night really was young. Like David Bachman, who downed two shots within two minutes. The man was twenty-five and ready to party, whether it was an appropriate place to party or not.

Sometimes Ken forgot he wasn't that much older than guys like David. *I may only be twenty-eight, but I'm almost the oldest of four rich assholes.* His brother Travis was only ten months older than him. Ken grew up with a work ethic and a respect for business so ingrained within him that the idea of being as emotionally immature as Mama's Boy David seemed preposterous. They felt at least ten years apart, not a mere three.

Then he went to a hotel bar, sat down at a small table to have a drink, and looked over to see a lonely blond woman nursing a martini. All maturity went out the window after that.

"Man, isn't that Lana Losers?" David asked, nodding in Lana's direction. She hadn't noticed them. She didn't notice anything but the TV playing the NBA finals. The Spurs were up over the Nets, something everyone in Ken's office would be pissing and moaning about come the following week. "Can you believe a woman like *that* is kicking ass in this gig?"

"I can, actually." Ken had a whisky highball to keep him company. He always preferred the stronger, earthier spirits after a long day, conferences or no. "We men underestimate women like 'that' every day." Lana shifted on her stool, crossing one slender leg over the other, black heels dangling from her dainty feet. She stood up straight when she wasn't hunched over her Blackberry. Occasionally a man slowed down behind her, either to check out her ass, hit on her, or both. Lana brushed them all off with a wave of her hand, as if bidding a bee to get the fuck away from her. More than one of those guys wandered off mumbling about what a bitch she was. *She has to be, doesn't she? Nobody takes her seriously, I bet.* They were probably like Ken – practically slobbering over her. At least he could rein it in and treat her like a human being when they interacted.

Not that he wanted to, mind.

A Fated Night

"Still, when was the last time a woman kicked that much ass? No wonder she works for Roger Prescott. That guy is so queer he probably lets her get away with everything."

"What does that mean?"

Either David was embarrassed or those shots were touching his cheeks. "You know what I mean, man."

"No, unfortunately." They may have only been three years apart, but Ken too often felt like an uncle to this young man. Which was silly, because he already had three nieces and nephews among his brothers. Meanwhile, Ken couldn't carve out the time in a day to even date, let alone think about kids. As a son in his family, that was sacrilegious… as he was reminded during every family gathering. "I can guarantee Ms. Losers has a hard enough time already. She probably doesn't need either you or me flirting with her."

"Hmm? So you fancy her?"

Yeah, the whisky was starting to hit. Or maybe that was Lana's radiance making Ken feel so much warmer. "What red-blooded heterosexual man *wouldn't* fancy her? I'm just not a slob about it. You shouldn't be, either."

"Admiring her. That's all."

"Admire her for her merits, not for her ass." Even though she had a fantastic derriere. *If she were my girlfriend, I wouldn't be able to keep my hands off it.* For the best she wasn't his girlfriend. "On that note, don't you have a girlfriend?"

"What? That means I can't look?"

"No, it means you need to mind where your eyes and hands wander before your cock follows. You're dating a Simmons girl.

Don't piss off either her or her family, for all of our sakes." The Simmons ran half of Brooklyn. There were so many up and coming neighborhoods in Brooklyn that Ken was salivating to get them on his listings. *I already know what agents I would assign to what properties.* Assuming David didn't botch the whole thing by cheating on his meal ticket of a girlfriend.

"How about you? You've been single for a while."

Single had such a loose definition. No, Ken did not have a woman he considered significant. Not in that way. He dated some women, but it never got farther than dinner and sex 90% of the time. Sometimes it was simply because he and his intended love interests did not click outside of the bedroom. Usually it was because Ken could not see himself putting any of his life on hold for these women. His career was getting started. Why would he jeopardize any of that for women who didn't inspire him to do better in the first place?

"Not sure what you're trying to imply," Ken muttered.

"Please, man, you look at her the same way every other man in this room is looking at her. You're going to tell me that you don't want some of that?"

"No. I don't want 'some of that.'" What a crude way to put being with a woman. As if she were a piece of meat to be consumed between two pieces of bread for lunch. Ken was into a lot of hinky shit, but he wasn't into *that* kind of play. What was with his fellow men and not knowing how to look at women as human beings?

So what if Lana Losers was the hottest woman in the room? Perhaps the hottest woman in New York City?

A Fated Night

So what if she was incredibly successful at such a young age, by her own merit?

So what if Ken was already calculating how he could pay Roger Prescott the headhunter's fee without looking desperate to both Mr. Lois and Mr. Bachman?

And so what if the longer he looked at Lana – from the back, no less – the more he wanted to run his hands up her sides and kiss the nape of her neck?

It wasn't that he was beholden to someone else. It wasn't that he didn't think she was good enough for him. It wasn't even that he was so single-minded at the moment that dating wasn't even on his radar. Ken had his reasons for staying away from Lana right now, and they had nothing to do with those facts.

"Don't you want her for our firm? I bet my dad would be pissed if he found out you had the chance to chat up the biggest agent in the region and didn't."

Ken glared at the young Bachman. *Seriously. How am I only three years older than this guy?* Ken would give David the benefit of the doubt and blame it on the shots. Not that Ken was bothered by the whisky he drank. All it did was make him feel more relaxed.

Lana finished her martini and pushed the glass aside, but not before pulling the olive out and absentmindedly sucking on it while watching the basketball game, one foot spinning in circles.

Lips as red as candy sucked that olive in a way a man could only interpret as *delicious*.

"Of course I want her for our firm, but we can't play our hand so early, David." Ken clapped him on the shoulder. "That would be silly. We let Prescott and Ms. Losers shop around a bit. Get to know our competition and what they have to offer. *Then* we swoop in with a better offer. Like the knights riding up to the castle to save the fair maiden from the terrible dragon."

David chuckled. "I thought you said we shouldn't look at her like that?"

Like how? Ken was staring at her again, admiring the way her hair slowly fell from her bun, making it messier and messier as the minutes went on. What did she look like with her hair down? Hell, what did she look like *naked?*

Damnit.

Ken picked up his glass. "You do have a point though, David. I should leave her with a good impression of us. On a personal level. That way when we broach something professional, she already has me – I mean us – on the brain." He stood, checking to make sure his suit was presentable to a woman of Lana's discretion. "Wait here, my good man. I am off to do some more networking."

David held up his empty shot glass. "I might take off in a few minutes. Good luck. Let me know how it goes, eh?"

"Doubtful it will go in that direction." Not that Ken would complain… but this wasn't about romantic intentions. This was business. Yes. Business. That's what Lana had come for, after all. Ken would have to honor that. Now, if she ended up moving to New York and still had a favorable impression of him? Ken wouldn't say no to a date then.

A Fated Night

He slipped into the space between Lana's barstool and the empty one beside her. Ken's glass lightly touched the bar. He pointed to her empty martini glass the moment she sat back in surprise at his immediate presence.

"Can I get you another one?" Ken flagged down the bartender. Lana popped the olive out of her mouth and tossed it into a crinkled napkin marked with the hotel's logo. "Or are you one and done tonight, Ms. Losers?"

Ken leaned against the bar. This made him a good two heads shorter than miss prim and proper Lana Losers, but what did he care? All the men in Ken's family were average height. They would never sweep into a room and tower over everyone else. Men who relied on that trick of genetics were only fooling themselves, anyway. Ken knew that not everyone took him seriously. Lana hadn't. The way she had looked at him when they first met was so dismissive until he introduced himself as *the* Kenneth Andrews. That got her attention right quick.

"I can get my own, thank you." Lana did not open her body language, but she also did not shut herself off to him. *Is that a good thing? That's a good thing, right?* Ken was not intimidated by independent women who knew what they were about and what they wanted. (Let alone had high standards. A woman of Lana's background, who had gone on to become a bit of a big deal in her own right? She had high standards.) He would, however, be quite disappointed if she shut him down before giving him a chance to talk shop with her. "Now, if you need a refill of your own drink, Mr. Andrews…"

Oh, he liked her.

Ken often found himself in a unique position. Whereas most of his peers only accepted one kind of woman into their lives, he appreciated a wide variety. Most of those same peers would have no idea that he was as likely to head down to the local BDSM scene and pick himself up a date to torment as he was to pick one up to torment *him*. Men in both the kink and professional worlds were expected to be Doms through and through if they had even the smallest drop of alpha in them. The business world particularly demanded it. *That's so boring, though.* Most of those same men would probably lose their minds to know that Ken would be open to Roger Prescott flirting with him. *Well, if he were my type.* He wasn't. Lana, on the other hand…

She was his type. Not only her stone cold beauty, but her fiery attitude as well. How much of this personality was a self-defense mechanism? How much of it was her true self? Ken was curious to find out.

Assuming Lana would let him in first.

"I'm still working on mine." He kept a respectful distance as he faced her and drank more of his highball. "Thank you, though."

Likewise, Lana spared him a few curious glances. "What can I do for you, Mr. Andrews? Did you come over to talk business or pleasure? Because I'm only in the mood for one."

Ah, yes. Ken had suspected as much. Lana was not here by herself to be flirted with. She was relaxing. Networking, as Ken had used as an excuse to come talk to her. That was fine. Not much fun, but *fine*. Besides, if she was going to come work for him in the coming months, Ken needed to make sure all his HR ducks were lined up in their proper rows. *What do I want most from this woman? For her to make me money? To pleasure me?* One type of relationship was much more lucrative.

"Then pardon me for interrupting, Ms. Losers. If you don't want to talk business, say so."

She scoffed. A long, intricate blond curl bounced in front of her face. While her roots were a darker shade of blond, Ken had no reason to believe that she was anything but all natural from head to toe. That only made her more intriguing in a world full of plastic surgery and fake platinum blondes who were convinced that nobody would buy properties from them unless they looked a certain way. Besides, Lana was from the Losers clan. Everyone knew that brood was as vane as a wicked stepmother from a fairy tale. *Even more intriguing.*

"Business." Her finger, tipped in bright red nail polish that matched her lips, attempted to straighten her curl. "Does Roger know you're talking to me right now?"

"Should Roger know?"

Lana offered him a dry look through cold, calculating eyes laced in a light, dusty brown. "Here I had thought you weren't interested in talking to me after how quickly you blew me off earlier."

"I had other business to attend to, but I have time to chat now."

Lana looked over her shoulder. So did Ken. Now, where had David Bachman gone? Gone already? Hopefully he wasn't out cheating on that Simmons heiress… "Unchaperoned?"

"Oh, please. I'm the chaperone in that relationship." Ken finished his drink. "David may be the owner's son, but I control more than that boy will understand." He looked into his empty glass. "Huh. How about that? Looks like I need a refill." Lana's empty martini glass clinked against his stouter one. "How about I get you that other martini after all?"

"Only if you let me buy you another highball."

"I believe they cost the same here."

"Well, how about that?" Lana waved to the bartender who responded with alacrity. "We'll both have a refill on our separate tabs."

The bartender picked up the empty glasses and disappeared to the other end of the bar. Ken reached into his inside jacket pocket and pulled out his favorite drinking activity. "Mind if I smoke, Ms. Losers?"

Her visage crashed into disgust. "Yes. That's foul." Oh. *Well.* Ken slowly put his pack of cigarettes back where they belonged. *I am suddenly aware of the lack of nicotine in my system. Great. So much for not being addicted.* "Besides, if you start smoking, Mr. Andrews, half the men in this bar will start smoking too. I would have to leave. You don't want that, do you?"

He cleared his throat. "Certainly not."

"Good. It should also sting you enough to know that you spoiled any chance you had of kissing me tonight. You should be ashamed."

***

A Fated Night

Lana lived for the abrupt shock hurled in her direction. *I'm cackling on the inside.*

She had known Ken Andrews was in the room before she stole a glimpse of him sitting with David Bachman. Since their first meeting, Lana hadn't been able to think about much aside from that man's presence. She felt it in the main conference room. Hell, she noted the moment Ken left to have dinner with some associates, for the room was suddenly devoid of that cool confidence that most men forced.

To think, she had come to this bar in the hopes of flirting with the bartender a little. Instead, she froze up like a popsicle the moment Ken entered the bar and emitted his powerful aura all over the place – and smacking Lana right between the thighs.

It irked her how handsome this man was. He removed his suit jacket and draped it across the barstool he did not care to sit on. That fitted vest was the kind of accessory Lana would love to run her hands across, admiring the hand stitching, feeling the luxurious materials, and then tearing it off a man's torso. What good was a man wearing such fine things if she couldn't destroy them with her sexual bravado?

Ken Andrews had no idea who he was flirting with. Lana wasn't some squeaky mouse playing in the big cat's pen. She knew how to hold her own with men like him. She had devoured half the guys who came by her all girls' school. Taken them to task at college, strolling right into the nastiest frats and leaving dazed dudes devoid of shame and semen in her wake.

Stormed through this office, that nightclub, dancing and flirting with anyone who struck her fancy. Lana wasn't compensating for anything, either. Her father had loved and doted upon her growing up. She had decent boyfriends who spoiled her with their money and bodies. No, the only excuse Lana had was that she loved to indulge in as many sexual experiences as she could have. At the appropriate time, anyway. This conference had not been on her list of *appropriate times.*

She also doubted that Ken Andrews cared to know any of that. The older Lana got, the more men were turned off to know what a *slut* she was. *Not to mention I'm getting to that point in my career where I have to watch my image.* What bullshit. Maybe a woman wanted to have a threesome at the end of a stressful week. Two men were preferable, but there were always couples at those swinger joints…

"You now have me questioning my whole adult life," Ken said with little of the shame Lana had told him to have. "How many women have I missed out on kissing because I smoked?"

"You really should question that. All men should." Only two things turned Lana off to the point she would drop a man like the hot potato he suddenly became. One of those was smoking. The other? She glanced at Ken's crotch. She couldn't tell from that angle if he would turn her off or not. "I'm living for the day they make smoking in these places illegal. Maybe some of us good patrons have asthma."

"Do you have asthma, Ms. Losers?"

She did a double-take at that smirk. "I should hope not." Would make her eclectic sex life moving forward a lot more

A Fated Night

difficult to enjoy. A woman couldn't very well have an asthma attack while getting spit roasted by two fine young gentlemen. Ruined the mood. "Why? Do you?"

"No."

Lana accepted her fresh martini. "So where is this business talk you wanted to have?" When Lana had said she was in the mood for only one type of conversation that night, she had been disappointed to hear *business*. She couldn't think of anything dourer. What was she? The real estate princess that everyone felt entitled to a piece of? *Yes.* In three days she would be accepting some trifle award to stick on her résumé. Sure, she worked her ass off to get that award, but she knew its shelf life in getting her on the roster of bigger and better firms was about six months. By that time her replacement (a man, probably) would be making waves along the eastern seaboard. *I wanted to either be by myself or flirt tonight.* She should've had room service sent up and consoled herself with a dirty movie on TV instead of coming down here. "I'm all ears, Mr. Andrews."

"Well," he began, distracting himself with a drink instead of answering her directly. *He has no idea. He came over here to flirt.* That knowledge almost made Lana smile. Ken was an intriguing man that she wanted to get to know better. Did he have a girlfriend? Probably. Men like him were considered catches of the highest order. *If he were my boyfriend, I'd lock that shit down.* Too bad monogamy sounded about as interesting as getting her toes waxed. *Ideally, I'd find a man who thought the same way.* "I have it on good authority that you're interested in ditching Prescott and moving up in the real estate world."

"Did you hear that from Roger?"

"Possibly."

Lana laughed. "It's fine to acknowledge it. We both agree that I need to move on. Works out for him if he can get a fee for my leaving, though."

"I'm sure."

The olive popped out of Lana's glass and into her mouth. She held tightly onto the toothpick while her tongue worked the pit out of its green casement. Right in front of Ken, she pulled the olive from her mouth and spat the pit into her half-empty glass. She wasn't going to drink that anyway.

The little show had the desired effect on the man next to her. Ken licked his lips without thought and turned his thighs away from Lana's line of sight. *That's right, Mr. Andrews. Think about me doing that to your cock.* Pleased with herself – and not for the first time that day – Lana folded her arms on the bar and bestowed upon him a coy look.

"You came to flirt with me, Mr. Andrews. Let's not skirt around that." Any man approaching her after a long day and many drinks in his system was going to have that on his schedule. *Flirt with Lana Losers: check.* Ken was bold enough to do it, and possibly dumb enough to cover it up with business talk. Too bad for him. Lana vastly preferred it when a man came right out and said he wanted to fuck her. She rarely had time for seduction. "Let's also not pretend that it wouldn't become a point of contention should I come work for you at Lois & Bachman. I don't fuck my bosses, gay or not." She had a feeling Ken wasn't *gay* if he was boldly flirting with her and

A Fated Night

trying to cover up the hard-on she was giving him. *Please. Look at how he's trying so hard to keep himself together right now.* Heat radiated between them. His skin. His breath. His heart pumping all that blood through his body – mostly to his cock. *Ah, heat cooking up in here too.* What a naughty boy. Lana had to admit, though, she had a particular addiction for how hot a man got beneath the shaft when he was about to erupt. "So what would that mean for my career prospects if I fucked you tonight?"

Ken's mouth fell open at that blatant question. Lana picked up the olive she never finished eating and tossed it into his mouth. The effect was immediate. Ken swallowed.

She did love a man who was willing to swallow.

Chapter 3

"Let's See Where This Goes."

Lana opened her hotel room door, tossing the key onto the nearest flat service available to her. She walked into the adequately sized space overlooking an equally adequate view of New York City and debated whether or not to close the thick curtains. How much of an exhibitionist was she, really?

Behind her, Ken Andrews closed the door, jacket hanging over his arm and hands stuffed in his pockets. Kinda cute how much he didn't know how to act around her. *I called him out on his bluff and then invited him up to my room "to talk."* It was also cute how he pretended to think about it before accepting. He even offered to pay for a bottle of wine to talk *business* over. It was already waiting for them on the table by the window.

A Fated Night

I'm either going to fuck this man or make him promise to hire me as soon as this conference is over. There could not be both. Lana was terrified of few things in her life. Being sexually – or, worse, *romantically* – involved with her boss was not only a HR nightmare but career fucking suicide. Nobody would ever take her seriously, and they barely did to begin with. *Ken would take me the least seriously of all.* Lana opened the bottle of wine and poured into both glasses provided. She smiled at her reflection in the window, especially when she saw Ken coming up behind her. Regardless of what direction this night went in, she won, either in the short term (sex,) or the long term (career.)

"Excuse me for asking you to come up here instead of going to your room, Mr. Andrews." Lana wanted to be in control as much as possible. At least she had some semblance of control in her own hotel room. *I know where my condoms are. I know where my laptop holding all my personal information is.*

Ken accepted one of the glasses of wine. His jacket threatened to slip off his arm and onto the floor. "Ken."

Lana held her glass up for a toast. There was simplicity to his name that was missing from most other men's. It was also ripe for a plethora of nicknames. *I like Kenny.* Even though it reminded her of Kenny Loggins, her father's favorite musician.

"It's no problem. I don't have a room here, anyway." When Ken caught the look of confusion on her, he continued, "I live in New York. I have an apartment a few blocks from here."

"Oh. Right." *How dumb of me.* Lana should have realized that she wasn't in DC anymore. "Well, either way, I appreciate you coming up all this way to talk to me, *Ken.*"

They toasted to the fate that had brought them together that day. Lana took a sip of the random red wine selected for their consumption that night. *A bit more bitter than I like it.* Maybe that was done on purpose. Maybe the concierge liked the idea of Lana Losers pursing her lips every time she drank in front of this man.

"You never did explain this phenomenon." He gestured to the gold rabbit nametag still on Lana's chest. *Idiot. Should've taken it off.* Ken was no longer wearing his nametag, so why should she? Not like she was going to be wearing this same jacket tomorrow.

"The organizers screwed up my name to the point it could not be recognized. This was Roger's idea of a last minute fix. Silly, isn't it?"

"Allow me?" Ken reached to touch the nametag on her chest. Before a flurry of tingles could make a fool out of her, Lana turned away, leaving the poor man's arm lingering in the air.

"I don't think so." Lana shrugged out of her jacket and draped it across the back of the nearest chair. "You haven't made your intentions clear enough for me to know whether or not it's a good idea you touch me outside of a handshake."

"Why, Lana," Ken said, admiring the sleeveless rose pink blouse she wore. It tucked effortlessly into her black pencil skirt, but that wasn't where his eyes lingered. *You like my tits? Trapped beneath this baggy thing?* Lana had half a mind to yank off her blouse and really give this man an eyeful. "I don't know what intentions I have left to make clear."

A Fated Night

"Business or pleasure," she called over her shoulder on the way to a leather loveseat. "You only get to select one, Ken." The moment she sat down, she crossed her legs, conveniently toward the other seat. The wineglass remained in her hand. *I'm gonna need more wine at this point.* "You don't get to have me for both."

"Now *there's* a conundrum." Ken was on his way to her, although taking his sweet time. Was it to give Lana a full view of his body? Because he walked like he owned the room. *My room. Don't get cocky, Mr. Andrews.* Lana did not hand her spaces over to anyone, not even a man she fancied. "That's like asking me what I desire more. Satisfaction in my heart or in my bank account?"

"If you're a woman, you're constantly searching for both."

"Aha." Ken dropped his jacket onto the arm of the loveseat and sat next to her. His aura was so palpable that Lana could lick it. *Bet he'd like that.* She did not miss the moment his legs also crossed – toward her. Their feet were willing to touch at any moment. "Either way, I'm up against quite the brick wall, aren't I? I mean, I was flirting with you. I think that intention is pretty clear."

"Say you want to have sex with me, Ken. We're both adults here."

The rim of his wineglass stayed pressed against his bottom lip. "Oh, I would love to have sex with you, Lana. Don't let that be misunderstood." He drank, his throat pushing two long waves of red wine down to his stomach. Lana had to look the other way before she burned like the rose of her blouse. "Also don't let it be misunderstood that I don't want you working for my company. Like I said. Quite the conundrum. Do I satisfy my current sexual urges for the short term happiness, or do I do the smart thing and hire you as my underling, always to remain professional to a fault?"

Ah, but he had walked into her logistical trap. *You said you wanted to fuck me, Ken. We can never go back from that.* Lana drank as much as he did. They had sexual chemistry. That had been established between them. *That would also follow us through our professional careers.* Again, what should she do? *Do I work for a man who wants me as much as I desire him?* Lana was not going to fool herself into thinking a real relationship could happen here. Even if it did, how long would it last? She would be the one cut from Lois & Bachman once the messy breakup occurred. *Messy because I refused to be the sweet girlfriend. Because I got bored.* They hadn't even kissed or touched outside of a handshake, and Lana Losers was already sabotaging a possible relationship.

"What do *you* want, Lana?"

She jerked her head back in his direction. "I'm not the one possibly fucking over his business."

"No, but you stand to lose the most, don't you?"

"Fuck you," she said with a snort.

"It's true, though. I won't pretend that it isn't."

Lana had no idea how that made her feel. She wasn't used to men, let alone her romantic partners, taking into account what happened to her once she left. *One of many reasons I don't get to have real relationships.* "I wouldn't have invited you up to my room if I wasn't at least interested."

A Fated Night

"Interested in what?" Ken leaned forward, wineglass dangling between his hands. "Come on, Lana. You asked me, now I get to ask you... do you want to have sex with *me?*"

Bastard. Dastardly, handsome bastard.

"Yes." Lana couldn't look at him. She didn't want to see the smug satisfaction oozing from his goatee. *My liking casual sex doesn't mean I don't have any self-respect.* Besides, that was so dumb of her to admit! Like he said, she had more to lose! Why did she admit that she wanted to sleep with him? Everyone would assume that he wanted to fuck her if she went to work for him. Not necessarily the other way around. Or so Lana wanted to believe.

Ken put his glass down. "Well, I suppose that solves that dilemma, then. Here I am, having admitted that I want to sleep with you. Here you are, admitting that you want to sleep with me. I'm in your hotel room where such things happen. Come on, Lana, you would've been disappointed if all we did was talk business up here."

Maybe. Ken's rich sensuality was the kind of thing Lana wanted to eat up – blind. *Tie that necktie around my eyes and make me explore you with my tongue, you bastard.* Was he into that sort of thing? Lana didn't think she could handle it if he were. *He would be too perfect. Gag.*

Oooh, gagging. That was fun too...

"We still could," she said with a haughty sniff. "Just because we want to fuck doesn't mean we can't speak hypothetically about what would happen if I came to work with you. You know, assuming we don't have sex."

He pushed his left hand against his knee, facing her with an incredulous look. "That's quite the head game."

I know, and I hate head games. She did love role playing.

"Come on." Her nipples hardened in her bra. *Christ.* What was wrong with her? She was better than this. She was Lana Losers! The woman who could turn it off and on at will! Or at least until now. What was this man doing to her? *Don't tell me I'm wet too. Don't think I could handle that truth.* "It's why we met, isn't it?"

When did her hand land in the space between her and Ken? When did he think it was a good time to touch her hand... and *not* for a shake?

Oh. God.

Lana gripped the armrest with her other hand. Her whole body braced itself for the intense rush overcoming it. One touch. *One fucking touch!* The man didn't even have huge hands, yet it was like they dwarfed hers! *I'm shrinking. That's the only explanation.*

"If you want me to go," Ken said, his voice deeper than Lana had heard it before, "I'll go. If you decide that the firm I work for is one that you would like to be employed at, I'll make sure this is never brought up again. It'll be like I was never here." The way his hand started to squeeze hers implored Lana to tell him to stay.

"Like you were never here?" she braved saying. "Don't give me that kind of whiplash. The moment you leave I'll be thinking of nothing but you." She looked away, although she did not reclaim her hand from his. "I'll go crazy with regret."

A Fated Night

"Well, then." Was Ken scooting closer to her? Yes. Of course he was. Lana could almost feel his breath on the back of her neck. What she could *definitely* feel was his hand letting go of hers and snaking seductively up her arm. Fingers as thick as whatever clogged Lana's throat pushed hair away from her ear, allowing Ken to whisper directly into it. "I don't want you to feel regret."

Her hand slipped across his thigh. Tight. *Hard*. The man did not want for a better exercise regimen. *Maybe he's not that much older than me.* Lana hadn't thought to ask. What did it matter? He could be twenty-five or thirty-five. All she knew was that she wanted him, and the bastard clearly wanted her.

Finally, she turned her head toward his, causing their lips to brush. Another spark set off like a tiny firework between them. *How cruel.* Lana really did not have a choice now. Business? It could never be. This man was already inside of her.

Yet.

Yet.

"Your move." Those words vibrated against Lana's lips. Her whole body *vibrated*. She could already feel his hands on her, squeezing her, caressing her, groping her hips and breasts as he did whatever felt the most natural. *Please don't tell me my fantasies are better than reality.* Lana couldn't bear it. Like she could no longer bear not knowing what it was like to kiss this man.

Her move, indeed.

Kisses weren't supposed to be silent. They were supposed to be loud, obstructive, and misophonic to everyone not involved. Those were the best kinds of kisses. Lana would sign up to get a kiss like that every day of her life. *Tongues everywhere. Lips crashing together. Moans and saliva out the ass.* So why was she losing her shit over a kiss that didn't make a single sound at all? Because it was with *him?*

Lana hadn't tentatively kissed a guy since she was thirteen and realizing that sex was a viable thing one could have for pleasure. *I'm no virgin about three hundred times over.* Yet it seemed right to only lightly peck Ken's lips, as if testing the waters of their chemistry was the best course of action. No jumping in. No being frivolous about two bodies making love. Something more stirred in the undercurrents of their mutual attraction. Something that made Lana open her mouth the moment she confirmed she liked kissing this man.

After that, it was like opening the gates to heaven.

Who really kissed who first? Lana opened the silent dialogue, but she may not have been the one to jump in before the other. Ken was as likely to be the reason they were now pushing against each other on the loveseat, hands on shoulders, behind heads, on chests and breasts. It wasn't a tiny peck anymore. It was a full-blown kiss that invited two people to come together and make utter fools of themselves.

Oh, God, yes I want him. Lana could barely keep herself away now. Kissing, touching… shoving tongues down each other's throats, for fuck's sake! *I'm a slut. I'm a total slut. I'm choosing to fuck this guy above having a professional business relationship with him that could make my whole career.* To be fair, he clearly wanted her too. Enough to break their kiss and say, "You're an unprecedented woman, Lana."

A Fated Night

His breathing was heavy, as if she had already given him a thorough workout. *You have no idea what I'm capable of, buddy.* Lana glanced down and saw her nipples poking through both her bra and blouse. Ken also noticed them with a smile. With that out of the way, he went ahead and showed her what that kiss had done to *him* by no longer hiding the bulge appearing between his legs.

Ah, damn. It was a nice bulge. Or so most women would think.

Lana was not like most women in so many ways. So many wonderful ways... but also so many unfortunate ways.

"Um," she began, tousling her hair while she fought to find the embarrassing words to say, "there's something I need to tell you. About me. And, uh, my body."

Ken suddenly wasn't quite as close to her. "What is it? Are you... do you have...? Because you might be pleasantly surprised to know that I would not mind."

He didn't say it, but the accusation was already there. "Oh, no!" Lana choked. "I'm clean, okay? It's nothing like that. I also have a vagina, thanks." Was she blushing? God, she was blushing! "Which is what I need to talk about anyway."

She had clearly lost him.

"I'm tight. Like... really, really, *really* tight."

Ken leaned back against the loveseat, eyes flashing between her face and lap at record speeds – as if he could see how tight she was.

"You may not think that's a problem..." There went her mouth, running off. *What am I doing? Keep kissing the guy! Give him a blowjob! Rub off on his thigh or ride his face or something if the whole penetration thing doesn't work!* Lana had been doing that for years. All the gynos she went to said she was a peculiar case, but that they didn't see an underlying cause for how small she was inside. Which meant she got to live her flourishing sex life with making sure nothing *too big* came her way, and that men on the larger side understood they couldn't just ram it in without causing them both serious problems… and possible trips to the ER. *I would die from the embarrassment!* Lana wasn't about to start that tonight, no matter how embarrassing it always was to bring up. "But it is. I have to be careful, or it could really hurt."

Ken's mouth twisted in either disgust or anguish… Lana could not tell to save her life. "So," he began, a frog dying in his throat, "no monster cocks, then?"

Lana giggled. Was that really funny? Or was she nervous? "No. Sorry."

"Well, I never thought I would brag about this, but…" His hand was back on her arm, fingers attempting to encircle her wrist, "I don't have a monster cock. You're welcome to inspect it first, if you'd like. Or we could do other things. Let's see where this goes."

Ken Andrews had to be one of the most affable men Lana had ever met. *I've met a lot of men.* Men from all over the world, with different class backgrounds, educations, and experiences. The only real difference between a man at twenty and the same one at fifty was that the older one couldn't get it up as often. *I can't even say they bite their tongues more often. Sometimes the man at twenty is a better gentleman!* Most men either froze up or instantly

A Fated Night

said stupid as fuck shit when Lana brought up her sexual issues. It was a great way to suss out who should stay and who should get the hell out of her sex life.

So far, Ken was both a gentleman *and* easy to talk to about these matters. Lana had to glance at her reflection in the window to make sure she wasn't blushing.

"Inspect it, huh?" More girlish smiles threatened to consume her face. She hid every last one of them behind her fingers, under the guise of scratching the bottom of her nose. "That's quite nice of you to offer. I'm sure your assets are perfectly acceptable."

"I am woefully average in many ways. No, never mind. I like to think I'm smarter and more ambitious than the average American male. Physically, though, my doctor loves to go on about how perfectly in the middle I am regarding many things. I am, however, average when it comes to other, more important things."

"Not including your intelligence and ambition?"

He grinned. "In spite of that, really."

Lana squeezed his thigh, her fingers brushing against the bulge hardening in Ken's pants. "Can I tell you how maddening it is to be a woman who loves sex but has this issue? I feel like Cinderella sometimes. Trying to find the right penis that fits my tight little vagina." She sighed through her red lips. "One day Prince Charming will come along and be a perfect fit. Hmph. Does this kind of talk make you uncomfortable?"

Ken shrugged, gaze transfixed on where her hand wandered. "Nothing makes me uncomfortable as long as you're touching me like this. You could tell me about your three nipples for all I care."

"I don't have three nipples."

"Dunno. I might have to inspect that."

Although it impressed her to have him talk so frankly about himself (because that's what a man's intrinsic confidence did to a woman) Lana had to wonder what the catch was. He couldn't be this self-assured. Either he wasn't *that* into her that the stakes were high enough, or he was harboring some terrible, narcissistic secret that would bite her in the ass. She hoped it wouldn't happen until after she curled her hand around his erection, holding herself back from squeezing too hard.

A Fated Night

Chapter 4

"But Do You Need Me?"

Only a single breath shot through Ken's nose when she touched him. Otherwise, he was the picture of cool and calm, the kind of man that Lana was quick to fall for when they were alone in the bedroom.

She hadn't even registered how he felt in her hand when she thought *I want this man to change my life.*

Oh. Now she registered how he felt. Lana comfortably wrapped her hand around his cock. Girth was what mattered most, after all. She could work with different lengths, as long as the cock's owner didn't think it wasn't real sex until he was completely sheathed within her. *I ain't that deep, buddy.* Width, however, had a nasty predilection for giving her a bad time. She could never relate to stories of overly thick cocks and how good they felt. *Sounds like my nightmare.* That didn't mean she couldn't *feel* as good, though. Lana would leave the big guys for her gal pals who had pussies that could stretch and accommodate to any dick under the proverbial sun.

"I hope it's satisfactory," Ken said with a sly look. "Because he's taken with you, Lana."

"That's nice, but is his best friend taken with me?"

Ken lifted his hand to her cheek. His touch was so delicate that Lana felt bad for squeezing him so hard in turn. *How much self-control does this guy have, anyway? Shouldn't he be throwing himself at me by now?* A guy who exerted that much control over himself was dangerous to Lana's psyche. It meant he was the best of both kinky worlds.

Damn. She was already thinking about kink? How fucked up was this whole situation?

"Anytime now, Lana." Ken lowered his hand to her breasts. Lana gave him a curt nod before he squeezed her like she squeezed him. Her breast filled his hand, her nipple fighting to break free and to touch his bare skin. "You can give me your answer anytime."

"What answer?"

His nose lingered against her throat. "Do you want me?"

What kind of question was that? The man was as hard as a diamond in her grip, and she wasn't letting go unless he told her to. He teased her skin with kisses full of fire. He slowly pulled aside the cowlick of her blouse and groaned in approval to see her wearing a pushup bra. *Not that I need one. The extra illusion is great, though.* Even she thought so.

A Fated Night

Yes, she wanted him. Lana had wanted him from the moment they met, although she didn't entertain the thought until he was sitting next to her at the bar. As soon as she had him in her room? Her body had quivered to have him in her intimate vicinity. "Hell yes I want you. Why aren't you fucking me on this couch already?" Saying things like that gave her such a rush. Seeing him grin in that bad boyish way made her high.

Ken's expanding aura pushed her against the back of the loveseat. Her acceptance of him had certainly emboldened him, hadn't it? *Oh, good. Because I'm feeling like an exceptional bottom tonight.* Lana could easily switch up the roles in the bedroom. Ken made her want to lie down, spread her legs, and take everything he gave her.

"Because I want to make sure you're good and ready for me." He flicked the spot where her nametag had been earlier. "Miss Bunny."

How flattering. "I'm ready."

"How can I be sure?" Ken left another kiss on her breast. "You've told me something very intimate about yourself. It's now my job to make sure you're wet enough to have me."

"I thought we established that you don't have a painfully monstrous cock." She was feeling it right now, wasn't she?

"We did, but I would be remiss to not take care of you." His hand slipped between her thighs like hers remained between his. "Remember what I said? We can do other things. I for one am a big fan of foreplay."

"Me too." Lana wasn't sure how much longer she could stand to touch this man but not *touch* him. Now that his face was in her cleavage, tongue pushing into her bra and attempting to get a harder rise out of her nipple, Lana had no choice but to encourage him. Her lips pressed against his forehead while she teased the tops of his ears and held on to the back of his neck. His goatee felt like soft down against her skin. When his tongue finally found its mark, Lana gasped, disappearing into the couch with a needy jerk.

"Relax," Ken said, his hand inching up her thigh. Soon he would find her slit, and then what? Would she combust in pleasure? Perhaps. At this rate. "Enjoy yourself, Lana. You've chosen me to be your partner in pleasure, and I plan to deliver. I deliver in *all* of my relationships, business or pleasure."

"I'll be sure to keep that…" Lana moaned as one ripple after another came with the strokes of his tongue. "In mind!"

They were doing this. They were *so* doing this!

"Yes," she cooed, mussing his hair with constant flicks of her fingers, "suck me off."

Ken sank his tongue deep into her cleavage, licking the sweat from her skin and leaving a trail of his saliva to collect in her bra. *Damn. Why is that so hot?* Lana continued to fall against the loveseat, or perhaps she was simply sinking farther into oblivion. Ken's hand found her slit, crammed hot and tight between her curvy thighs. Two fingers rubbed her lingerie against her folds. How hot was she? How wet? And why wasn't she touching him where it mattered most? Where had her hand gone?

To his zipper. If there was one thing Lana subconsciously wanted to know the most, it was whether or not Mr. Andrews

A Fated Night

was cut. Not that it mattered either way when it came to her pleasure. She was merely nosy.

"I should be asking *you* to suck me off," he said with great candor. Every word muttered against her skin like a pleasurable cataclysm setting off into the stratosphere. "Your lips have been haunting me all day."

Lana had naturally plump lips. Even when she didn't accentuate them with her makeup, they still turned men's heads. *Every guy in the room is always thinking about me sucking his cock.* Not surprising that Ken would be the same way. He was a guy with a cock, after all, but that didn't bother Lana when she was getting into bed with a man. She *wanted* to suck cock. Life had such few great pleasures like that.

But Ken wasn't going to give her that opportunity anytime soon. He was shadowing her on the couch, encroaching into every inch of her personal space, forcing her to accept him into her arms. *Okay.* Lana embraced him, kissing his forehead as hard as her large lips would let her. "Hot damn you're turning me on, Mr. Andrews."

"You turned me on long ago, Ms. Losers."

"For the love of my sanity, fuck me."

"It would be my pleasure." He dipped his finger and thumb into her bra to give her nipple a hard, titillating pinch. "And yours, hopefully."

Ken stood up first. Even though he was physically away from her, Lana still breathed his air and inhaled the musk emanating from his body. *Fuuuuck, I want him. I want him so badly I might make a fool of myself if I'm not careful!* Lana accepted a helping hand to get off the couch. For some reason she thought it pertinent to fix her scrunched pencil skirt on the way to her hotel bed. Always about appearances, even when they didn't matter much anymore.

"Come here." Ken stopped her halfway across the room, holding her head close to his so he could kiss her without struggle. The dastardly way he planted his lips on hers was almost too delicious to conceive. Even though it was a seemingly simple closed-mouth kiss, Lana still reeled from it. *No man has kissed me like this before.* Not even the suave devils who thought they were God's gift to women. Oh, hell, especially them. They were a fake kind of bravado, anyway. Ken was the real deal. That had to be why she was nervous, even though she refused to let it show. *I don't want him to think I don't want to do this.*

The closed-mouth kiss turned open-mouth. His tongue pressed upon hers, unmoving. Was that how he thought of her right now? Was it a sign of what he had in mind for her? *Push me down, hold yourself on top of me, take what you want...* Lana would not oppose.

"I think I have made the right decision," he said when he turned away, hand lingering in hers as he continued to lead her to the bed. "About business versus pleasure, that is."

Lana remained standing by the edge of the bed even after Ken sat on it. She straddled his bent leg, the strength of his muscular thigh splitting hers apart. She wanted to kiss him. Hold him to her. Grind her cunt against his leg and make him feel the heat she spilled for him. But Lana could practice a good amount of self-control too. Enough to taunt him with a slow and deliberate undressing of her body – and his.

"I have no regrets thus far." Lana pulled her rosy blouse over her head and tossed it onto the floor. Ken braced himself against the bed, eyes wide and glued to her chest. *Someone is a breast man.* Not every man could be pigeonholed into one of many categories, but Lana definitely knew how to play up a breast man, a leg man, an ass man, or, God help her, a *foot* man. Breasts were the easiest. Almost always at eye level. Ready for heavy petting and a killer pair of lips. It helped that she wore one of her favorite bras that day. Extra comfortable. Extra voluptuous.

"You get hotter by the second, Lana." He couldn't help himself. Even though it meant a loss of balance, Ken tugged on the little strip of fabric holding her two bra cups together. Lana didn't need that distraction. She was busy unbuttoning this man's vest and the shirt beneath. "I'd have been a fool to not have come up here to fuck you. I'd have regretted it for the rest of my life."

"You're fluffing up my self-esteem, that's for sure." Lana slowly pulled her thighs up his leg once his vest came off.

"Good. I vastly prefer women with high self-esteem."

So you can tear it down? How unfortunate that was Lana's first thought. "Do you have a condom?"

Some of the life came back to his eyes. Whatever he had been fantasizing about had crashed into the pit of his stomach once reality came knocking. "Yes. In my wallet." He glanced at his back pocket.

"That's dangerous, you know." Lana Losers, woman on the prowl and sexual educator of all men, reached into his pocket and pulled out his leather wallet. The initials KSA were carefully etched within a royal fleur-de-lis design. *What's his middle name? Samuel? Seth? Solomon? Steven?* Lana opened it, pleasantly surprised to see the man kept his things meticulous. Cards. ID. Cash. (A lot of it.) *Stephen. I was close.* Good for him for having a decent driver's license photo, and good for him for having a separate slim container to keep a condom in. Not only was it more discreet, but it was a smart way to protect one's prophylactics. Lana pulled out the condom and tossed Ken's wallet onto the floor. She didn't care about the other junk.

"Why is it dangerous?" Ken finished unbuttoning his shirt on her behalf. "Getting cold feet?"

"Hardly." Lana slipped off his leg, hand remaining on him. It moved effortlessly into his pants, drawing out his hard cock for her to admire. *Damn, that's nice.* Big enough to entice her, but not *too* big to scare her off. *Goldilocks is pleased.* Finally, she had found one that was just right. "I'm so warm I can't stop thinking about blowing you." The carpet called to her knees, a siren's song that would lead her mouth to his stiffness. *I can taste his precum already.* Her favorite. "Trust me, you've never had a woman do it like I do it."

"Hmm." Ken gripped her arms, preventing her from getting down on her knees. "No."

"No?" What? That was new, and annoyingly different. Maybe a girl wanted to stick a cock in her mouth and go to town! "Something you need to tell me?"

A Fated Night

"Yes." Ah, that was a much better word. Even better when it included Ken wrapping his arms around her and pulling her down on top of him, her thighs lowering mischievously toward his. The closer she got to his cock, the closer she came to nirvana. "I want inside of you, but not like that."

"Oh?"

She fell over with a mighty *jumpf!* Ken loomed over her, a dangerous look clouding his eyes. *Oh, my.* "Yes, *oh.* You can't tease me with facts about your..." Suddenly his hand was between her legs. Lana opened them wider, air filling her lungs the moment his fingers made contact with her slit.

"About my what?"

"What do *you* want me to call it?"

Lana grinned. "My cunt and I are as good as friends as you and your cock. See? Those are fun words to say."

"Indeed they are." Ken pulled off his shirt. Lana pressed her hands upon his chest. Hard. Strong. Surging in breaths. "Anyway, as I was saying..."

"Yeah?" Lana hiked up her skirt so she could open her legs as wide as possible. *Make no mistake, Mr. Andrews, I want you to fuck me.* "What were you saying?" *Say those dirty words and make me wetter.*

Ken snatched the condom from where Lana left it on the bed. "You can't tell me about how tight your cunt is and *not* expect me to fuck that first."

He sat up, easing both his pants and boxers down until he stood in nothing but his skin. Clothes may have made the man, but Ken Andrews was no stranger to his nudity. He moved as effortlessly, as confidently as if he still had clothes on. *How much of this confidence is coming from his cock?* It was ready for her. Stiff. Tip dripping in precum, and all he did was look at her. His sack was rather impressive beneath that tuft of dark, curly hair. More of that hair trailed up his abdomen with the lightest dusting of it on his chest. This man groomed. A lot.

She thought he would lunge for her. Instead, he carefully removed her underwear, forcing her legs to come together and then split apart again. Ken's eyebrows arched up when he found himself unexpectedly gazing into the core of her body. *Like what you see? Extra pink, for you.* Lana was quite familiar with what she looked like down there.

"Can't decide if I should take this skirt off of you or not."

"Too much effort." At that announcement, Lana pulled her skirt up to her hips, bunching it into wrinkled bits within her fists. Ken guided her legs around until her head was on the nearest pillow. The man had an image he needed to see: Lana Losers, spread eagle in her pushup bra and hiked up pencil skirt. Her makeup had yet to smear, so her lips were full and red and her eyelashes daring him to ravage her. Her hair was already mussed and only acquiring more tangles. *Wait until he fucks me.* With any luck, she'd need a good hour to get the sex tangles out of her hair.

Ken knelt between her spread legs, one hand clasping the base of his cock and the other freeing the condom from its wrapper. *Anytime now, Mr. Andrews. Fuck me for the first time.* The first time was always the best. Or the worst. Lana had a feeling this was going to be *the best*.

A Fated Night

"You know what's hot?" The condom crowned his cock. The man was deliberately taking his time unrolling it down his shaft. He didn't even look at it. His eyes were locked on Lana, drinking in her curves, her hair, her makeup, and most definitely her scent. "You."

"Oh, such a way with words." Lana opened her arms to accept him into a carnal embrace. The head of his covered cock rubbed the inside of her thigh. "I thought you were going to comment on my cunt."

"Not yet." He kissed her, tongue dipping into her mouth, sinking slowly, *slowly* toward her throat. Breath passed from him to her. It relaxed Lana, which was what she needed. Because no matter how badly she wanted to be with him, there was still the matter of biology. *Nothing is worse or more embarrassing than being gung-ho about sex and then having things clench up too tight.* "Give me a moment and I'll provide a full review."

"Be careful. Don't hurt a girl's feelings."

Ken tested her entrance with the head of his cock. *Shit, shit.* Lana focused on pleasant things, like the way he looked at her, nothing but a cool calmness on his visage. "Ready?"

Such a sensual voice. Asking that simple word was enough to make Lana writhe like a madwoman at the height of her pleasure. "I've been ready. I can't stop thinking about what you're going to do to me."

One inch entered her. Ken momentarily dropped his façade that said he was unaffected by whatever they did. *He's so affected.* That was an aching relief on his face. Enough of one to compel Lana to touch his cheek and coax him to kiss her again.

The deeper he entered, the deeper his kisses became. One sweet, agonizing inch for every twist of his tongue against hers. Lana was a glutton for both. *I want him everywhere at once.* Her body welcomed him, her own ache sated by the tender strokes of his cock within her. She moaned into his mouth and swallowed him, hungry for more. Ken waited until he was all the way in before slowly rocking against her.

"Fuck," he groaned into the maw of her opened mouth. "You were right. That's... *tight.*"

You're telling me? She wasn't even about to come, yet her core clamped on the man's cock as if it were ready to milk him dry. *The best fucking feeling.* "Too tight?"

"There's no such thing." He diverted his mouth to her shoulder, lightly sucking her skin and leaving the pinkest mark behind. "How's it for you? Okay?"

"Okay?" Lana pushed her hips up, wanting *more.* "I'm fucking fantastic, skip." She clung to his shoulders and bent her knees. The slight shift in the angle of penetration granted them both what they wanted. Lana's little cry of pleasure was only rivaled by the grunt in Ken's throat. "Fuck me. *Please.* I'm ready."

"But do you need me?"

"Yes!"

"Thank God." He wrapped both of his arms beneath her and thrust, hard. "Because I'm about to lose my mind. I need this too."

Lana knew a lot of things about sex, but she had no idea what it felt like for a man of any size to fuck her. Not just his

A Fated Night

physiology, but hers as well. *How tight is too tight? Am I not deep enough? Will I hurt his feelings if I have to stop because it hurts?* What a time for her insecurities to manifest! Poor Lana wanted to enjoy herself. What woman wouldn't? She was in bed with a handsome man who made her feel at ease, let alone *good*.

Did Ken feel good right now? Was it exceptional? Mediocre? *Stop doing this to yourself! You're supposed to be having sex!* Why was Lana even dwelling on this? She rarely obsessed over how a guy felt while fucking her. Why was Ken so different?

Indeed... why was he so different?

Was it his skill? His careful way of entering her, hitting her where it created the best sensation, and pulling back out again? Ken's hips thrust in a steady rhythm that was both blissfully predictable and mesmerizing. *Fuck me, fuck me, fuck me...* Lana loved it. His perfect thickness that filled her without hurting her; his virile groans muffling her moans as he kissed her; his strong hands either pinning her to the bed or tenderly touching her sensitive skin. Lana opened her legs until she had him as deep as she could take him. Ken's breathing increased. His hands slapped against her hips, holding them down so he could fuck her. Lana used the opportunity to slip her hand down her slit and find her swelling clit. She wasn't the only one beginning to swell. Ken's cock grew thicker, but he had gone at her enough that her body stretched to accommodate him.

She tried to speak, to tell him how good he was and felt, but nothing came out of her but exceptional moans. The music of the room consisted of a squeaking bed and grunts from a man who collected sweat on his brow.

"Are you gonna come for me?" Ken held his cock within her, coaxing her to take the full extent of him and what he offered. "You gonna come on my cock, Lana?"

"Yes..." It was exquisite torture, feeling him pound her core until she grabbed the sheets and begged him to keep fucking her. "Fuck, yes!"

Her back arched when he resumed his thrusting. Sure enough, within ten more seconds of taking him any way he dictated, Lana came.

All she would remember later was the mattress digging against the back of her skull, the air stealing from her lungs, and this hard, greedy man claiming every little bit inside of her. Lana slammed one hand above her head and scratched at his shoulder with the other. Wherever she was, it was not on Earth. It wasn't quite Heaven, either. Heaven implied that he was coming with her, cock contracting, spilling its contents into her while the man made primal noises in his throat. Ken did not do that. He held back, for whatever reason. He forced Lana to experience her climax all by herself, grunting, writhing, becoming a hedonistic demoness who was intent on taking this mortal man down with her.

It ended as quickly as it slapped her across the face. Lana exhaled a deep breath before accepting another kiss to her dried lips. The man still had plenty of vigor within him. What to do about that?

Fuck him again, of course.

The walls were down. Lana knew she could handle him. Better yet? He knew how far he could push her. *Apparently he*

A Fated Night

can push me quite far. Good for him. Ken had managed to get on top of her and give her a solid orgasm from his cock. (The kisses and the tit-squeezes helped as well.) Yet now he had unleashed her true nature – and Lana Losers did not stay beneath a man for very long.

"Whoa!" Ken soon found himself on his back, his erection now covered in Lana's orgasm. *How about another one?* Her hair created a curtain around their faces when she kissed him and ground her hips against his. Her stretched, aching hole begged her to find his cock again. She had been filled. Why wasn't she still? "Damn, you're sexy."

"Not so bad yourself." Lana could growl too. In fact, Ken had no idea how much of an animal she could transform into. Once she sat firmly in his lap, his cock spearing her very core, Lana ripped off her bra so she could properly enjoy gravity and what it did to a woman's breasts when she was riding a bucking stallion.

Ken's eyes whirled in increasing arousal. How was he not coming yet? Lana kept waiting for it, but he never came. Damn. How good was he at holding back? *That good? Is he one of those guys who purposely delays orgasm when he jacks off?* Bless those guys. When Lana was in the mood to ride cock, she was in the *mood.*

"I'm so happy that I'm inside of you right now." The boyish laugh in his voice also implied as much. "If only you could see yourself right now."

"I've got a good enough idea." She could see her reflection in his eyes. No, not her full reflection. But she could tell that he thought her painfully beautiful sitting on his cock and pushing her hands against his chest. "You better come this time. I want to know what your cock feels like when it reaches the point of no return."

"It feels great."

Lana languidly stroked his shaft with her inner walls, squeezing him, tormenting him with an inner power most men didn't know she had. Ken's eyes found themselves closed, his mouth perpetually open and hands floating in the air. *That's right. I'm that good.* Lana took him to the hilt and made herself as comfortable as possible. "*You* feel great."

"Prove it."

Oh, Lana would.

She threw herself into some void that could not be penetrated by any outside force. Once she was in it, there was no going back. Men often spoke of the exact moment they knew an orgasm was unavoidable. Lana felt much the same way when it came to sex. Except her point of no return lasted as long as five minutes sometimes. *I don't want to leave this headspace. I don't want to abandon nirvana.* She had an amazing man trapped between her legs. Why the *fuck* would she leave that?

So she rode him. Hard, desperately, taking complete control of how fast and how intensely he entered and filled her. When orgasm began to reappear, she clawed into his shoulders again, thrusting herself back onto his cock while her clit grazed his abdomen and the soft hairs growing right beneath it. Ken timed his upward thrusts to meet her downward ones.

Ah… there it was. It had been a false alarm last time. Ken hadn't been on the verge of coming back then. He was on the

A Fated Night

verge of coming *now*. So happened that Lana was relaxed enough to take whatever she damn well pleased in her tight cunt.

"I'm gonna come," she announced. Her breasts were pushed in front of her arms, and her hands reddened Ken's chest from how hard they pushed against his skin. "Fuck me until you come too. Don't stop. Don't..."

Damn, another one clobbering her in the back of the head.

Lana didn't know what the hell she said when orgasm first broke, but she didn't care. She doubted it was coherent anyway. Just a mess of sexual curses that implored her to impale herself on this man's cock and take everything he had. *Mine, mine, all mine, everything related to this cock is mine.* The man, the rigidity, the seed coursing through his cock and doing its damndest to fill her up. All of it. *Ken* belonged to her. Maybe not outside of this bedroom, but certainly in this moment, in *her* bed.

She would make sure he knew that he was hers. Her nails scratched his skin, leaving claw marks down his chest.

Lana's euphoria lasted longer this time, but it was a sweet paradise she lived in. The satisfaction she felt, not only physical, brought her slowly down from the deepest parts of her mind and let her rejoin Ken in the here and now. After letting out a laugh of carnality, she fell forward, covering Ken's face in girlish kisses. He grabbed her ass, pushing aside the hem of her skirt in favor of feeling nothing but skin against his.

They remained like that, Lana hovering above him and offering kisses that carried a wind of familiarity. How much time passed? Lana didn't know. Perhaps it was an hour.

Perhaps it was ten minutes. All she knew was that Ken did not topple her off him until he was good and ready to leave her body.

"You're amazing, Ms. Losers," he said with a husky post-coitus voice.

She chuckled in his arms. "That was worth not getting to work with you."

He neither agreed nor disagreed. He kissed her instead, quite pleased with what they both managed to accomplish that night.

***

Lana awoke to a sunny New York morning after a fitful night of sleep in Ken's arms. Or at least she assumed she spent most of the night wrapped around him. Hard to tell when a girl conked out faster than a truck with a busted motor.

Also hard to tell when a girl woke up alone.

Not surprising, though. Her clock said it was almost ten in the morning, and there were at least two voicemails from Roger on her little Nokia clamshell phone. Lana held the phone to her ear and listened to her boss ask her where the fuck she was... they had a brunch to get to.

Ken undoubtedly had other important things too. More important than spending the morning with his conference lay. *Whatever.* Lana had been enthralled with him last night. Today was a new day. She would get over him by the end of the conference.

A Fated Night

Or so she told herself until she rolled over on her *other* side and saw a folded card sticking up on the nightstand. A brand new conference pass – with her correct name and agency, no less – was beneath it.

"I took the liberty of having your makeshift nametag replaced. Although I'll miss the rabbit. See you around, Miss Bunny. Perhaps we'll chat again before the conference ends."

Ken had elegant handwriting. Not quite cursive, but more slanted and tied together than print. Every letter was distinct, with large capital letters starting every word and smaller capital letters following. Lana flopped onto her back, holding the card above her face and smiling at her lover's penmanship. Maybe she would keep it as a souvenir of their night together.

"Yeah, Mr. Andrews," she said with a yawn. "I'll see you around." Now, what should she wear to the second day of the conference?

Chapter 5

"She Has A Wicked Tongue."

The current meeting Ken found himself in was indescribably grueling. Which was strange, because he rarely gave a shit about shooting the breeze with his industry peers under the guise of having a serious business meeting at the region's biggest conference of the year.

Yet every word coming out of these people's mouths were like nails on a chalkboard. They had nothing interesting to say. They didn't inspire him to take action in his own business. He spent more time correcting their misconstrued facts about the current state of the real estate bubble and less time taking notes about new enterprises he may wish to pursue. It didn't help that everything was couched in empty terms like "synergize."

A Fated Night

Times like these made Ken Andrews go back to fantasizing about what he really wanted to do in the future. *If Lois & Bachman think I'm staying with them until retirement, they're idiots.* Ken had dreams. Aspirations. Those dreams and aspirations called him to start his own company and cut out the middle men. The bosses. The higher-ups that told him what to focus on and for how long. He wanted to diversify his properties. There were millions to be made in flipping older properties into new ones. Why wasn't he spending his precious free time on those pursuits?

Oh, right. Because women.

Hello, Ms. Losers. That was his immediate thought when Lana entered the main reception room and went up to a bedraggled Roger Prescott. She was 100% pleasant while he berated her for being so late. *Ah, she's late because of me.* A man had to take pride in that.

Ken's night with Lana had been a grand success. As much as he wanted her on his roster, he wanted her wrapped around his cock even more. She was so right. They could not work together platonically after what happened the night before. The chemistry had been there. They acted on it. Now it was amplified ten-fold, keeping his eyes locked on her as she briskly walked across the room to join another group of conference goers.

She briefly met his gaze, tucking her long blond curls behind her ear. Her lips were not as prominent today. Didn't matter. Ken could easily imagine kissing them. He could also imagine tearing that white, green, and blue mosaic dress off

Lana's gorgeous body and having his way with her again. *That chair. Right there.* Ken had to cross his legs as he let his imagination briefly wander to thoughts of fucking Lana over the back of a large leather chair. He hazarded a guess that she was even tighter in that position.

Damn. She hadn't lied about that. From the moment he entered her, all he could think about was how great she felt on every inch of his cock.

"Hottest piece of ass in the room, huh, Andrews?"

Caught staring, Ken tore his eyes away from Lana and met Carl Jefferson's as he sat in the empty leather chair. Carl, with his heavyset build and penchant for young blondes he could pay to be his girlfriends, was undoubtedly having similar thoughts about Lana as Ken was.

And Ken did not consider himself the jealous type. This was a man who was once more than happy to setup a gangbang for his girlfriend of the moment when she shared it was one of her biggest fantasies. Turned out she couldn't handle the emotional aftermath. *"You weren't even a little jealous? What's wrong with you?"*

So this made no sense. Why would he feel a twinge of jealousy in the pit of his stomach at the thought of other men wanting Lana like he had her. *One night stand, brother.* Well, maybe they could do it again, but he was under no delusion it would be anything more than a summer fling. Lana lived in DC. Ken lived in New York. They were both too busy to date under those circumstances, even if they had an open relationship.

A Fated Night

An open relationship? Am I nuts? Why did he automatically assume Lana would be up for that? Just because a woman could be as sexually entertaining as she was…

Ken forced himself to focus on Carl. "Excuse me?" he said, pen clicking in his hand.

"That Lana Losers." He said it like the word *losers*. It made Ken cringe. There was nothing losery about Lana. *Too bad about the last name, though.* "She's the star of the conference, all right. Every heterosexual man in this dump is craving that cunt of hers."

Jesus, Carl. This was a man with six sexual harassment lawsuits under his belt, so Ken couldn't be surprised. He would have to be cordial, though. Carl was an old friend of the senior Bachman. "So I guess that leaves her boss Prescott out."

"Never thought I'd see the day I was glad to have a homo around." Carl was the only one laughing at his inappropriate jokes. "Speaking of Prescott, though, I hear he's looking to sell Ms. Lana to the highest bidder. I thought flesh peddling was illegal."

This man was a laugh a minute. "From what I understand, Ms. Losers," he made sure to say her name correctly, for her sake if no one else's, "has outgrown Prescott's agency. He'll make more money off a headhunter's fee than he will keeping her in a place like DC."

"Pah. Virginia. Unless she hops the border and starts selling in Chevy Chase, she's useless both to herself and every firm in the area. I can't lie, I'd love to have her on my roster." Carl licked his lips. Ken wanted to gag. "She needs to move up to

New York. The question is, who's gonna snatch her up and make both her and themselves millions?" Carl looked back toward Ken. "Are Lois & Bachman interested in her?"

Ken closed his notebook and shoved it into his conference folder. Surrounding him were other men and their assistants typing up panel notes into clunky square laptops that started smoking after fifteen minutes of use. Ken had recently seen some prototypes for flat handheld computers that a man could use with a slide out keyboard. It sounded too good to be true. (It was. His friend in the tech industry told him that they were still a few years away from the public market.) Apple was particularly interested, but only if they got their flat touch-screen phones off the ground. Ken didn't know if he would be able to give up his Blackberry, but he'd try.

"I'm sure my bosses would love to pursue a talented saleswoman like Ms. Losers." Ken removed his reading glasses, folded them up, and stuffed them into his vest pocket. "But I don't think I'll be pursuing her on their behalf."

"Oh? Why the hell not? You a mad one?"

Ken snorted. "Hardly. I don't doubt her skills." A woman that charismatic and flirtatious could sell a humidifier to a Floridian. "I just don't think she'd be the best fit for Lois & Bachman. I have other enterprises to pursue."

"That so? Well, all the more luck to me, then. Perhaps I'll speak with Prescott about it later. Think she'd work for seventy a year before commissions?"

That's underselling her, but you knew that already. Asking her to move to Manhattan on top of that? For only seventy-thousand

A Fated Night

a year? Ruthless. Lana couldn't be that stupid to take an offer like that. "You should ask her."

"Oh, I will. Then I'll ask her to dinner, eh?" Carl's laugh wasn't much better than his manners. It certainly didn't compare to Lana's sweet giggles. She could come off as a cold woman, but when they were alone, Ken was able to hear a completely different side of her. *I wouldn't mind getting to know it better.* Ah, so not meant to be.

"I'll sweeten the pot with my own personal bonus, if you know what I mean." Carl stood and nearly knocked the coffee table between him and Ken over. "Pardon me. Thoughts of beautiful women, you know!"

There's no way your cock is bigger than mine, Carl, but you tell yourself that. "I do know what they're capable of, yes." Ken spared him a diplomatic smile before Carl took off to speak with someone else. When Ken looked for Lana, he could not find her. Just as well. He didn't want to slip back into inappropriate thoughts, no matter how sweet they seemed in his head. Lana deserved better than to have every man in the room drooling over her – and that included him, the man who had his cock pumping inside of her the night before.

***

Carl Jefferson was not the only man with ulterior motives toward Lana, as Ken unfortunately found out as the day went on. More than once he heard the underlings of this agency and the head gentlemen of that one discuss the grand achievements the woman accomplished during her short career. Then they talked about what they wanted to do to her in the bedroom. Or the shower, if one particular pervert could be believed.

Ken could hardly stand it. When he wasn't being abruptly reminded of the amazing sex he had with her the night before, he was subjected to that curdling jealousy embroiling his heart in war. *Settle down. She's not your girlfriend.* How else could he feel when half the men at the conference openly talked about wanting to fuck her when she wasn't in earshot?

And Roger Prescott… the fucking *idiot*.

He knew what he had on his hands, and he knew how much money he could make off Lana at the end of this conference. He was practically her pimp, touting her to one agency only to turn around and play up *other* strengths to yet another firm. Everyone he talked to was interested in Lana Losers, the sexy she-devil who had managed to sell half of the DC suburbs in the past year. "She has a wicked tongue," Roger said to Carl Jefferson. "If you know what I mean, sir." Carl grinned into his iced tea to hear that reference.

It was disgusting.

Ken knew he wasn't much better in some ways. He readily admitted that. Wasn't he the man who had gone up to Lana's room the night before with the hopes of having sex with her? Then did a mental fist pump when he cleaned up in the bathroom afterward. *I mean, I am only human. Of course I wanted to have sex with her. Of course I was plenty pleased with myself when I got to come inside her – and made her come twice.* Point of pride right there.

A Fated Night

It wasn't that other men were attracted to her that bothered him. It was the way they discussed it, treating it as an open joke of the conference. Lana Losers had arrived the seller of the year and would soon leave the sexual laughing stock of New England real estate.

Not her fault. Not her fault she was a gorgeous woman who could charm the habit off a nun. She worked both to her advantage, but the men who surrounded her should have known better than to treat her as if those were her only skills. And Roger! He played right into these men's fantasies, coyly suggesting that he knew of Lana's raunchy personal life. If the man could be believed, Lana spent most of her weekends at sex clubs picking up male submissives and having threesomes with swinging couples. *Honestly, that's too good to be true.* No woman was that perfect.

He had an hour break in the late afternoon. Although he was due back to attend a soiree – that included more damn networking – Ken made an effort to step out into the New York streets he called home. Initially he intended to take an extended smoke break, but the moment he pulled out his lighter he remembered the disgust on Lana's face. The image turned him off from his cigarette. Instead, he decided to channel his nicotine-craving energy into walking around a few blocks and perhaps running some errands.

A street vendor at one busy intersection was selling a plethora of trinkets alongside the common assortment of papers and magazines. Ken waited for the long light that would lead him straight back to his apartment. Occasionally he glanced over at the brass lockets swaying in the hot summer breeze. One in particular caught his eye. A little brown rabbit.

Well, now, that wasn't fair. It was almost like the universe was trying to tell him something. But what, though? Certainly it wasn't trying to convince him that fate had somehow brought him and Lana Losers together. Rabbits were a common motif for almost everything. It didn't mean anything at all.

So why did he buy the cheap trinket with only the most well-appointed thoughts in his heart?

***

Ken rechecked the manila envelope before he slid it across the concierge's desk. "Make sure Lana Losers gets this, please." He left a fifty dollar tip on top of it. "Before seven, if you can."

The concierge on duty covertly snatched the envelope off the counter. "Certainly, sir. Would you like to include a note?"

"There's already one in there. If you must have a sender's name, tell her it's from KSA. She'll know who that is."

"Absolutely." The man in his slick department store suit smiled at Ken while he filed the envelope into an outgoing mail bin. "Thank you for your patronage."

"You're the one doing me the favor, I assure you."

Ken walked away, checking his watch to gauge how much time he had before a panel on compounding interest economics began. He hoped to see Lana there. He was disappointed to not see a single head of blond, let alone that luscious mosaic dress, present at the panel. Such was the nature of conferences.

A Fated Night

Chapter 6

"I Want A Conference Fling."

A staff person presented Lana with a small manila envelope as she was entering the elevator to go up to her room.

What now? She didn't have time for this. Roger wanted her at some cocktail hour to schmooze with various New York honchos. She was *tired* of it. *I thought I came here to attend workshops to better my craft… and to accept that shiny award, of course.* Instead, Roger had her doing a fucking press tour in the hopes of garnering millions of dollars for her blond head. *I hate you, Roger.* He would make her rich in the long run, but right now she hated him.

So what the hell was this?

Lana stole to the back corner of the elevator while tourists and other conference goers crammed together in front of her.

She had enough room to open the envelope and take a peek at its contents.

A necklace spilled into her hand. Lana almost dropped it between herself and three other people, each smelling of body odor at the end of a hot June day. *That was close.* What was it?

A rabbit? What in the fuck?

Paper slid out behind the necklace. She instantly recognized the block print penmanship of Ken Andrews – her heart skipped a beat, and she swore she smelled his subtle cologne.

"Ms. Bunny - Ditch your plans for the evening and head next door to the other hotel. Eight o'clock. Present the necklace to the front desk. They'll know what it means."

Lana looked around the elevator. Only one nosy old woman looked back at her. "Slut," she swore the woman mouthed.

"I want to talk to you. About business, this time. Not between us. Just about you. Something you should know before you decide who to work for next. -KSA"

The elevator stopped on her floor before anyone else's. Lana stepped out in a daze. What would she tell Roger?

***

Turned out Lana was too ill to go to the cocktail hour that night. She accidentally ate something she was allergic to at lunch, and now it was wreaking havoc on her stomach. Or so she told Roger over the phone. He was upset, of course. He told her to hang a pine tree air freshener from her ass and get it

A Fated Night

down to the cocktail hour. She told him some harrowing details about what she had done to her hotel bathroom – that shut him up.

There was only one other hotel next to the one hosting the conference. A smaller, more historical one that foreign dignitaries and senior citizens on vacation were likely to use. Certainly not big enough to host a conference larger than a dozen people. Still, it was a quaint place, an updated gothic splendor that made Lana feel right at home the moment she stepped into the well-lit lobby at ten to eight.

She had changed clothes after taking a shower. Gone was the mosaic dress that made her stand out. Now she wore a crimson spaghetti-strap cocktail dress made business chic with her black Chanel blazer. Lana stopped in front of a glamorous mirror by the front desk to make sure her ponytail was clean. One curly lock licked her face. Satisfied, she approached the front desk and opened her clutch. Lana produced the brass bunny necklace to the night auditor on desk duty.

"Ah, you must be Ms. Losers." The young man's customer service smile was well practiced. "Follow me, please."

Lana had no idea what to expect. Ken had said this was about business, but that could've been a lie to get her alone again. *That man must still want me.* She sniffed, smug in the knowledge that no man could only have one taste of her. To be fair, she was pining for a small sample of him again. She had simply assumed she wouldn't get it.

They did not enter an elevator or go upstairs, however. The night auditor led Lana down a back hallway toward the small and intimate conference rooms. A reserved sign decorated the one at the far end of the hall. One knock of the night auditor's knuckles opened the door.

Ken was already there, sitting at a four-person table overlooking the indoor pool. Lana recognized the two-way mirror almost instantly. Even if a guest decided to take a quick swim before the pool closed, she and Ken would still have privacy.

He got up and shook her hand with pure business decorum. "Lana. Thank you for joining me at the last minute. Have to say I wasn't sure you would come."

The night auditor pulled out her chair for her. Both she and Ken sat back down, her host of the evening asking the auditor to have a server bring them a wine and cheese plate. After being thanked, the auditor left them alone in the small conference room.

"Of course I came," Lana said. "I had to know what this was about."

She treaded the line of professionalism and flirtation. After all, she didn't know why Ken had invited her here. The man ordered wine and cheese for a snack, but they were in a conference room, not a bedroom. The signals were so mixed it was a good thing she wasn't coming in for a landing.

Even if that landing was his lap.

"I promise not to take up too much of your time." Ken leaned against the table, his black and white Glashutte watch enticing Lana to gaze at the strong hands that had touched her whole body the night before. *We're both mature adults. We can*

A Fated Night

handle this. "I know you're busy. Everyone with an agency in the tristate area wants you on board."

Hmph. He had no idea. Lana thought she would have to work harder to get these good ol' boys to hire her on to their firms. So far she felt like a princess whose hand was up for marriage to the highest bidder of a neighboring kingdom. Daddy Roger would want pure gold for her golden head at this point. *At the end of the day, I decide where to go work, but he'll try to influence me based on his own interests.* Lana wasn't stupid.

"Yes. I am busy. Yet I took time to come see you when you requested. A man who claims to no longer want to hire me."

"I thought we established not to mix business and pleasure."

"We have. Glad you're honoring it." At this rate, Ken Andrews was the one person at the conference Lana could relax around. The most he might want from her was companionship. That wouldn't be terribly hard to deliver after knowing how he could do a girl. "What's this about, then?"

Ken leaned back. The wine and cheese plate arrived. Red wine as bitter as it was sweet hit Lana's palate with brie cheese squares. Lana didn't want to mention she hadn't had dinner yet. The cheese would have to sate her until she could order room service.

"You're not going to ask why I had you come meet all the way out here?"

Lana shrugged. "Because we fucked last night and you don't want the whole conference to know." If they were caught having a conference like this at the original hotel, people would talk. At first they might assume they were doing business, but Lana knew she was a sexual specimen to be talked over if there ever was one. "Such an honorable man." She picked up another piece of cheese and tapped it against the table. "My only other piece of curiosity is wondering why *this* hotel. How did you secure a room like this at the last minute? Why, Mr. Andrews, do you have a friend who works here?"

His cunning smile went nicely with his dark facial hair. "You could say that. I own this hotel."

The cheese piece crumbled between Lana's fingers. "What?" she asked in disbelief. Him? Owned this hotel? On Fifth Fucking Avenue? He had to be joking! He may have been the lead manager at Lois & Bachman, but he did *not* make that kind of money unless…

Unless…

He was already filthy rich even without the prestigious title.

"That's right. I own this prime piece of real estate. Got it for a steal a year ago. I'm a firm believer in spreading out my investments."

"I… wow." Lana knew her real estate. That included her Fifth Avenue real estate. Even if Ken got this for "a steal," it still had to cost at least tens of millions of dollars. Possibly a hundred! *Okay, maybe not that high…* "What are you doing working at Lois & Bachman? You could afford to run your own firm!"

"This is the only piece of property like this that I own. I'm testing the waters, so to speak. I don't have many concrete dreams, Lana, but having a wide real estate portfolio is one of them. And yes, I am definitely considering running my own firm when I feel that I am ready. Although ideally I would like a partnership with someone who can complement my skills. Haven't found that person yet."

"Impressive." Lana had dreams like that too. *One day, when I work my way up to the top, I'm going to own my agency and tell people like me what to do!* Lana was fantastic at sales, but she was even better when in control of every little detail. "I'm saving up my money to buy some hot properties too. There's a bubble coming and I want to get in before everyone else does."

Ken's eyes widened. "That's what I keeping saying." Apparently the topic change was a pleasant one for him. *Why did I come here again?* Did it matter? "Diversification is important. Housing is good here, but I worry about what's looming on the horizon. Same with business buildings. Hotels are a safer bet at the moment."

"Why don't you run this place?"

"Oh, no. I'm not interested in running buildings. I want to own them and reap the benefits. I hire other people to do the bullshit for me." The man had a sexy wicked grin, Lana had to give him that. "Perhaps I'll flip it to someone who would rather get into that sort of thing. I hear the Mathers are always looking for more hotels to command."

What a curious man. An ambitious man, too. *Ambition is like a drug for me.* Lana had some tough life lessons under her belt when it came to men and their ambitions. She was attracted to masculine courage. Except most of the men she gravitated toward for something more serious turned out to be complete idiots with their courage. Ken was one of the most careful men she had come across in a while. *Dang. I legit have a crush on him now.* First he was good in bed, and now this madness? Heresy.

"Anyway," Ken said with a cross of his legs. *Is he getting turned on too?* This was turning dangerous. "My main reason for inviting you here has nothing to do with my personal holdings and plans. I wanted to let you know something. About the grapevine around the conference."

Lana perked up with dignity. "Good things, I hope."

"Let's say you truly are a popular woman. To the point where I would hate to see you get lured down a dark path."

She furrowed her brows. "I can assure you that I know what I'm about."

"I didn't mean to suggest that you don't, but men talk. Behind women's backs." Ken fondled the stem of his wineglass. *We drank wine last night and then had some of the best sex ever.* Lana could still remember how firm and wonderful he felt between her legs, whether he pinned her down or she rode him to a second orgasm. If that was what he could do with his cock, then what could he do with his fingers and tongue? A woman wanted to know. For science. "Many firms are interested in hiring you. Their goal isn't only to use you for money, though."

Something uncomfortable settled in her stomach. "They want me for my body more than my mind. That's not hard to figure."

He studied her reaction for a long time. "Indeed. Not just your future coworkers. Your future bosses as well. Please be careful, Lana. Be very selective in who you choose to work for."

She snorted. "Is that what you brought me here to tell me? That men are sexist pigs?" Lana shot him another look from across the table. "I'm well aware of that. Like I'm well aware you would be a nightmare boss and want me for the same reason your colleagues are bragging about wanting to fuck me."

"Yes, I admit it," Ken was quick to say. "If you worked for me, Lana, I wouldn't be able to stop thinking about you." His elbows were back on the table, face coming closer to hers. "I'd make a fool of myself with my lust for you. That's why I could never hire you."

At least he was honest about it. "Not even for your future firm that is sure to take over New York?"

"Absolutely not. The only way that could work is if I married you."

Lana almost dropped her wineglass.

"Then I could fuck you whenever I wanted without it coming between us professionally."

He said it so candidly! As if he had said he wanted roast beef for dinner!

Stunned, Lana sat back in her chair and decided he was joking. That was the only way to deal with it.

A very hilarious joke.

She laughed.

"Do I amuse you?" Ken asked.

Lana took a final swig of her wine. *Last time we had wine together... we had sex.* Was this a sign of more things to come?

And come? And *come?* "Admit it, Mr. Andrews. You invited me because you wanted to be alone with me again. Like I don't know most of those men entertaining me out there only want me for my tight cunt. That you took for a spin last night, nonetheless."

"Indeed I did." Bless him, he was trying so hard not to react. It was almost cute.

"You want to do it again. Admit it."

Ken cleared his throat. "I wasn't going to. That wasn't my intention for asking you here."

"So what was? To make sure I knew how hot I was? How sexually desirable you men find me? Honey…" She was enjoying this too much. "That's not news. Everyone but Roger Prescott wants a turn at this. I'm going to pick the best firm based on what *I* will get out of it. You don't want me for your firm because you've fucked me. That's fine. At least you're honest and trying to do the right thing. Makes me want to work for you." Her smile was genuine. "Almost."

He looked away before tentatively meeting her eyes again. "What do you want, Lana?" he asked with a low voice. "Just tell me."

She leaned across the table, taking his hand. 'You own this hotel, right? That's damn sexy." When she received another incredulous look, she veered back on topic. "I want a conference fling. That's what I want. I want the only man who's not going to hire me to fuck my brains out. So get us a room here, Mr. Owner. You're not hiring me for business, but I'm hiring *you* for pleasure."

A Fated Night

***

Ken had no idea how they had quickly degenerated into this again… but he wasn't going to question it.

The moment they entered the suite upstairs, he and Lana were on one another. Kissing. Touching. Dry humping like a couple of teenagers who didn't know what they were doing. *Fuck that. I know what I'm doing.* The suite door latched shut, and Ken pushed Lana against the nearest wall.

"Ooh," she purred. "The tiger comes out to mate. What are you going to do to me, Ken?"

He slammed his mouth upon hers, shutting her up with the added bonus of tasting her wily tongue. *She tastes like the bitter agony of rough sex.* His favorite kind of agony.

"I'm going to fuck you sore," he promised. How lovely for the second night in a row he got to pull her skirt up and tear at her underwear. "I'm going to ravage you until you don't know anything but screaming for more."

"*Fuck,*" Lana muttered. "That's what I'm talking about. Are you going to do it now?"

Ken was too drunk on her body to immediately respond. "Hell yes I'm going to do it now."

He pulled her farther into the room. *Damn, I am hard.* The ride up in the elevator had driven him insane. Lana was so woefully beautiful in her red dress and black blazer. Her come hither lips and eyes taunted him the whole way up, daring to imply that she wanted him as much as he wanted her. *Impossible, honestly*. Who was Ken? Another guy at the conference. He figured that he was more likely to jack himself off to sleep that night than to ever fuck Lana again. She said so herself. They were a conference fling.

Yet they had now reached the second day in a row of fooling around.

Ken had yanked off his jacket and vest by the time his ass hit the bed. He thought Lana was right beside him, but he was mistaken: she was kneeling on the floor, her bright eyes locked on his as she dove for his zipper.

"You didn't let me last night," she pointed out, like his cock pointed at her the moment it was freed from his pants. "You've gotta let me now."

Oh, like he would turn such an offer down!

Ken Andrews was living the absolute dream right now. He owned this hotel. He owned this *room*. All he had to do was say the word to the front desk, and he was guaranteed whatever room he wanted. On top of that? He had the hottest woman at the conference – the woman every man wanted to fuck, as she so eloquently put it – on her knees and flicking her tongue against the head of his cock.

The way she sucked him was so greedy that Ken had to briefly wonder if he was dreaming. *No* woman did it like that unless she was so enthralled with a guy that she didn't know any other way to live.

Holy. Shit.

Lana's mouth wasn't much bigger than other places in her body. While she easily took his cock into her mouth, it was

A Fated Night

such a tight fit that Ken worried he was going to come too soon from the sensation. *Control yourself, man.* The heat of Lana's mouth surrounded more than his shaft. It pressed into him, warming his stomach even when she wasn't touching it. Her blond hair called to him like a beautiful beacon. "*Grab me. Now.*" Ken obliged as his cock slipped completely down her throat.

Had a damn blowjob ever felt so fucking good? Ken thought he had some great ones before, from both women who were experienced and finding their way around a dick for the first time. Lana, though? Everything she did screamed *skill*. This woman wasn't shy around men. She was as willing to devour them as they were to devour her. *Me. That's me tonight. I'm going to devour the fuck out of her.* She sucked, he fucked, together they made a delightful mess.

"Shit," Ken uttered in a long, drawn out whisper. Lana's tongue lashed against the underside of his cock, his tip pressing against the back of her tight throat. She squeezed his base and massaged his sack. This woman wanted his cock in her mouth so badly that she was willing to choke on it. *Don't choke.* That would preemptively end their fun.

Although at this rate, Ken was about to end something else.

"Okay, okay." It took more than a little coaxing to ease her off him. His cock sprung from her mouth, ripe with attention and dripping in fluids. His, hers, both. "That was amazing."

"I barely got started!" Why was she so indignant about it? Was she trying to show off? "I was going to let you come in my mouth. In fact, I was looking forward to it."

Oh, I bet. Ken would've loved that, but he had other things he wanted to make sure he did. Starting with pulling out the condom he put in his wallet when he got home the night before. "Maybe later. I need to fuck you. Like, *need* to." His hands were shaking on the wrapper. Lana grabbed it and ripped the condom free. Her excitement made him hurry to take off more of his clothes.

The condom slipped easily down his shaft. Once it was on, Lana kicked off her underwear and climbed onto the bed. "Do it," she said, pushing her ass into the air and showing off her tiny wet slit. "Pound me. Now."

Yes, ma'am. Ken always did enjoy a woman who knew the right way to order him around.

His hands were on her ass before his cock breached her center. Lana cried out in what Ken could only describe as *perfect tension.* She was wet. So wet that her arousal had to have started all the way down in the small conference room. *God, she wanted me that long ago tonight?* Had she been thinking about him all day? How quickly could he get his cock in her?

Not quickly enough. Lana was looking at him with rabid desperation. "Do it!" She further turned into a mess when he grabbed her by the breasts and squeezed. "Fuck me!"

This was so unlike last night and yet exactly what they both apparently wanted. Lana practically shoved herself back onto Ken's cock, forcing him into her and stretching her in ways she was probably not ready for.

"Fuck!" she cursed, face contorted into that mess of pleasure and pain some people craved. "Come on! Don't stop!"

A Fated Night

How could a man say no to that kind of plea? As soon as he had his bearings, Ken plunged deep into her.

Just like the night before, Lana was so tight that Ken's cock felt like it was trapped in the most seductive vise in the world. Yet she was also dripping wet, her thighs slick and her inner walls working Ken's cock farther into her. Her fingers turned white from gripping the bed. Her snarl of sexual reverie turned him on even more. Her ass flexed beneath his gaze, a pretty pucker calling to him to put one finger in. Maybe next time.

"Spank me," Lana whimpered. Her core sucked Ken right into it, and soon it would be drinking his seed if it wasn't careful. "Please!"

He obliged. Her skin quivered beneath his heavy touch, the sharp smack of flesh on flesh louder than Lana's moans of pleasure.

"Again! Spank me and fuck me 'til you come!"

What had gotten into her? What had turned her into such a sex fiend? How could Ken put off his orgasm so he could torment her some more?

As if he could. He was so wrapped up in the erotic images surrounding him that he almost managed to ignore the expert way Lana massaged his cock within her. Because, yes, she was totally doing it on purpose, and Ken was going to give her what she wanted, whether he was ready to go or not.

So he might as well get a few spanks in.

She jerked against him every time he smacked her ass. "Fuck! Yes!" She was thrusting back against his hips faster than he could thrust into her. "Fuck me!"

Lana came so quickly that it almost caught Ken off guard. But before he knew it, Lana was tighter than ever as she slammed herself against the bed.

Heat retracted from his sack and into his shaft. This was it. Ken had two seconds to completely let himself go and enjoy what his body was about to do.

Sweet, sweet relief blew from his whole frame from his cock. By then he was so deep within her tight cunt that Lana groaned incomprehensible sounds to bear it.

Yet there was no greater relief than falling down next to her on the bed. Lana rolled onto her back and sidled up next to him. She was wearing more clothes than Ken, yet she exuded a vulnerability that rivaled his. Only then did he truly realize that they had one helluva quickie.

"Wow," he muttered. "Where the hell did that come from?"

Lana chuckled against his arm. "When I know what I want, I get it."

Vicious. And completely admirable. Ken had many moments like that in his life as well. "You wanted me? That badly, huh?"

"What can I say?" Lana pulled aside his open shirt and lightly kissed his exposed shoulder. "You turn me on."

"The feeling is mutual."

She propped herself up on her arm and gazed down at him. Her free hand gently massaged his thigh. Not to arouse him again. Pure affection. Something Ken had been missing in his life lately. "You're not a woman to be underestimated."

A Fated Night

"I should hope not." Her fingertips traveled from his pectoral to his abdomen, following the deep crevices of his body lines and awakening whatever had yet to go completely dormant after an orgasm as hard as the one he had. "That would be dreadfully boring."

Ken shifted his body more toward hers and propped the nearest pillow up beneath his head. *What in the world are my employees stuffing these pillows with?* Something to talk about with the general manager. "You don't strike me as a woman who can stand to be boring."

"Yes." Lana relaxed against him. More vulnerability. How many people got to see her like this? How many men, specifically? Ken would hazard a guess that not too many men saw the sweeter side of Lana. "I mean no. I mean..." She laughed. Such a light, airy laugh that no one, least of all Ken, would ever guess came from such a slim frame. "I have no fucking clue. Why? Do *you* like boring?"

"Not particularly." Two could play her skin tingling game. Ken gripped her thigh, nails brushing against her slickness. *I did that to her. Good job, man.*

"So it's settled. I'm not boring." Lana, already devoid of her black blazer now that she was in bed with him, went an extra step and unzipped her dress with a pretty contortion of her arm. Ken obliged her by pulling both of her red spaghetti straps over her shoulders. *So beautiful.* And soft. And delectable.

"You certainly aren't." Ken kissed the curve of her throat. Lana, still shrugging out of the bodice of her dress, intercepted his lips for a more subdued kiss.

Ken was of two minds right now. His first thought? Lana had called him her conference fling, and the damn thing was already halfway over. *I could have her for two more days.* A good length for a summer fling. If Lana was up for it, she could easily become one of the great lays of his life. God knew they had enough chemistry to make them simmer in their own mutual admiration.

But his second thought lingered on something more. Something... magical.

Because that's what he swore he felt when she kissed him like that. *Magic.* Her lips opened and seducing his. Her tongue gliding effortlessly along his teeth and then dipping farther in to flick against his tongue. Her breath injecting him with new life. Her silky little moans enticing him to keep kissing her, because she clearly felt this magic too.

"You're a good kisser," she murmured on his lips.

"It takes two."

Lana abruptly ended their kiss and huffed at him. "Why did you give me a cheap rabbit necklace?"

What? Oh, right. Ken had done things that day that hadn't included this. "I saw it and thought of you, Ms. Bunny."

"Keep calling me that and I'll start thinking it's my name."

"You mean it isn't?"

She mussed a small section of his goatee. "So you thought of me. Bought me a cheap trinket. Invited me to your personal hotel nobody knows you own. Immediately bring me up here and fucked me within five minutes."

"To be fair, you asked me to."

A Fated Night

Lana finished lowering the top of her dress. *God spent a lot of time creating her* She wasn't wearing a bra. One was built into her dress, but it had barely contained her round breasts. *Nope. Can't resist.* Ken kissed the top one, finger and thumb teasing her thick nipple. *This is why we had to quickly have sex first. Otherwise this moment would not have been possible.* "I could ask you to do a lot of things, Kenneth." Lana surveyed the way this man lavished her with affection like a queen surveys her domain.

"I am your willing slave, my lady."

"Mm." Lana fell back, breasts jiggling to Ken's great and masculine amusement. He followed her, cupping one breast from beneath and rolling his tongue around her areola. Her nipple was so stiff he could have sucked it dry for an hour. *Maybe I will.* "Be careful saying things like that around a woman like me."

He shot her a heated look. "Maybe I want to find out what happens." He also wanted to find out what happened when he inhaled as much of her breath into his mouth as he could.

Turned out it only had a minor effect on her. Lana bristled in pleasure, but her hand remained in his hair and her breath did not skip a beat. If someone wanted to talk about self-control, all they had to do was look at Lana Losers right now. "Most men don't want to really know," she said in a careful tone. "They joke about it, but they don't want it."

"I don't joke about those things."

Lana curled her arm around his shoulders, coaxing him to come up and kiss her properly. When that momentary fervor died down, she said, "I've yet to meet a man who doesn't."

"Lana," Ken said, gripping her as if she were a precious possession in need of keeping. *When this conference is over, she's gone, off to work for some dunderhead who doesn't know how to properly take care of her.* It wasn't fair. Why couldn't he charm her into his bed *and* his office? Lana was brilliant and ambitious. She was hot, too, which made her a seriously dangerous trifecta in the real estate world. Lana was the exact type of woman Ken lusted after for his life. "I'm a fan of communication. That may shock you, but also like you, I have extensive history with the same types of people that you do. Trust me when I say that there are many women out there who joke about that sort of thing too. I'm tired of it." He kissed her again. "Many men too, yes."

The woman who had so recently stolen his heart studied his expression with renewed interest. Did she see his meaning in his eyes? Or did he hide it too well? *Men, women, a lot of it's the same when it comes to getting what I want.* Yes, in the bedroom.

"You're bisexual," Lana finally said. Curiosity kept her interest piqued.

"I don't subscribe to any labels. Not like that." He curled some of her hair around his finger before tucking it behind her ear. Those bright eyes never stopped studying him. "It's too complicated." Gay, straight, bi… they all sent the wrong message. Gay disregarded his love for all things women and his ultimate desire to marry one. Straight didn't do justice to the occasional man he enjoyed the company of. Bi? That implied a lifestyle where a man could be a serious partner in his life – outside of business, anyway. That wasn't happening. "But I've been with men. Does that trouble you?"

A Fated Night

"What? No way." She was almost a little *too* enthused. *Aha. I found one of those.* Young Lana Losers probably spent a lot of her downtime reading and writing certain forms of literature that starred few female characters. "I'm trying to figure you out."

"Why? Thought I was a convention fling."

"You *are*, but that doesn't mean I don't want to hear more about the men sucking your glorious cock." She chuckled to see the condom still wrapped snugly around him. Dexterous digits rolled it off and deposited it into the nearest trashcan.

"How about the other way around?"

Lana's words jumbled with a start. "You fuckin' with me?"

"No." A few awkward memories entered Ken's mind. Then a few *non* awkward ones. A lot of awesome ones. Ken finished playing with Lana's hair and pulled her closer to him. "How about you, Ms. Losers? Fancy the occasional same-sex attraction?"

A sheepish grin enchanted him the moment it came within two inches of his mouth. "We're probably on the same page in that regard. I've been with women."

"Sexually?"

"Yes. Sexually."

"Wow. You really are the perfect woman."

He meant it as a joke, but Lana didn't laugh. "I wouldn't call myself bisexual either, though. I much prefer men." A touch as gentle as it was intense graced his shoulder. Too bad he didn't have any kinks in that shoulder to get out with her great massage. *No, just kinks everywhere else.* Mostly in his mind.

"I can't think of any occasion where I would happily be with only a woman. It's more fun when there are... others... ah."

Ken had touched her nipple again. "Others? Do tell. Because I agree." Outside of a few dalliances during his more experimental years, Ken's opinion on the matters of same-sex attraction was that they were best served with beautiful women on the side. He'd happily interact with the right man, but he got off the hardest if it was for a woman's enjoyment.

Lana whispered in his ear, "So much group sex, Mr. Andrews. You don't even know."

"Oh..." His grip on her side hardened – and that wasn't the only thing hardening. "I'd like to see that." Jealousy didn't play a part in those fantasies. Even if there were something more serious between them, the thought of Lana enjoying the pleasurable company of more than one person... well, it seemed like all was right in the world.

"Maybe you will see it one day, Mr. Andrews." Lana rolled away from him again, her legs swinging over the edge of the bed. At first he feared she was leaving him, but was pleasantly surprised when she further disrobed her clothing. The dress hit the floor, and Lana Losers was as naked as the day she was brought into this wonderful world. "Seems we're into some of the same, shall we say, events? Perhaps I'll sign up for a gangbang at a sex club and you'll be one of many men cumming themselves to come cum in me."

That had to be the best tongue-twister Ken ever heard, and she executed it flawlessly. "Gangbang, huh? You're a busy woman."

A Fated Night

Lana pulled back the covers on the bed. Good. She was making herself at home in his hotel room. *I should've taken her back to my place, but I couldn't wait.* Tomorrow, perhaps. Lana was the kind of woman who deserved to be impressed, and Ken couldn't think of a better way to impress her than by taking her to his luxurious modern apartment. *I want her naked like she is now, spread across my bed and begging me to fuck her again.* Ken had equipment in his home. He wondered if Lana would be interested in something like *that*.

"I'm pretty busy, yes. You should see my planner." She tugged on the covers beneath Ken. Oh, right. He should join her. "Gangbang every Friday. Threesomes on Sundays. I take Saturdays off to be a slut with only one person." She welcomed his naked body against hers. "Guess that's you right now. Every day is Saturday at the moment."

He couldn't stop himself from kissing her once their skin slid together. Every part of her was as soft and responsive as the last. "I like Saturday."

"Hmph." Lana acted put out, but she did not ask him to stop kissing and caressing her. In fact, she was practically on top of him, one leg cast over his hip and breasts shoving into his face. *Excellent. Much easier to get to them from here.* "You're not going to ask me what I really mean by that?"

Honestly, Ken didn't care. He was distracted by how good he felt with her. Perhaps it would be fleeting, but he would commit to memory, so if fifty years went by and he still wasn't happy? He could remember a time when he felt the closest to happy... ever.

"What do you mean, Bunny?"

The next few words she intended to say were clipped right out of her mouth. Was it something he said?

"That was adorable." Lana opened her mouth and inhaled his lips. Next thing Ken knew? Lana was on top of him, grinding her hips against his and oh-so-kindly asking that he get hard again. She desired to know what it was like to have him come in her mouth.

He agreed that a mutual sharing of oral talents should take place. Now.

Chapter 7

"Everyone's Talking About Her."

Lana was in a daze from the moment she woke up in Ken's arms until she returned to the conference and had a hard dose of reality smack her in the face.

Too bad, too. Lana's sojourn to Ken's hotel (and she could still not get over that a man like him owned a whole hotel) had been like escaping into a fairy-tale. Well, Lana's version of a fairy-tale, anyway. She didn't care about being treated like a princess, or encountering magic at every turn, or feeling like she was in epic, romantic love. She cared about getting fucked hard by a hot guy. Having that same guy then become the cuddler of her dreams was a tender bonus.

What she didn't expect was thinking as fondly of the cuddling as she did the sex. All three rounds of it.

Men were rarely worth hanging out with after the deed was done. This was one of many reasons Lana did not seriously date a man often. Too much effort. Too much drama. Too *much* of the same thing again and again. Oh, she casually dated many men, but as soon as things took a turn for the monogamous, she was bored. That boredom usually started long before going steady was even on the table.

Ken was not boring. Not yet, anyway. There were more layers to him than Lana's last birthday cake, and she was only getting started licking away the icing. *He's so confident in his sexuality. He has so many career ambitions. He's diversifying!* Lana knew she was approaching thirty when a guy diversifying his investment portfolios turned her on.

He was also kinky. The last time they had sex, she asked him to hold her hands above her head while he fucked her. *"I can do you better. Come to my place tomorrow evening. I want to take you to dinner and then really get in that head of yours. Tell me every dirty thing you like, Lana."*

In a perfect world, he would be a perfect boyfriend. But it wasn't a perfect world, as Lana unfortunately rediscovered when she joined the conference after making a quick trip up to her hotel room.

Word had spread about her. Idle boy gossip, she was sure, although Roger probably played a big part as well. Lana couldn't walk five feet without someone from this agency or someone from that firm implying he could make her rich beyond her dreams. Only half of them followed that statement up with a promise to make her happy in more than one way.

A Fated Night

Ken was right. Lana had known he was right before he said anything, but that didn't mean he was less right. Besides, it made it feel more official when she had outside confirmation and it wasn't pure conjecture brought on by a woman's paranoia. (Not that she didn't have anything to be paranoid about, to be sure… but one of Lana Losers's greatest faults was her inclination to completely give in to her paranoia and engage in self-sabotage.)

Perhaps it was even worse that it was a man of his standing who noticed it and felt compelled to warn her. To what end? Out of the goodness of his own heart? Ken had made it clear he had no intention of hiring her for his boss' firm now that they had established a sexual relationship. Even so… wasn't it in his best interest to steer her away from his competitors? Assuming he really was impressed with her achievements?

Ah, there it was. The paranoia rearing its head. If she wasn't paranoid about her appearance, she was losing her mind over her job or her love life. See? This was why she dumped one over the other two. It wasn't worth fretting over all three when two alone were enough to make her lose her mind. So she would say goodbye to the serious love life in favor of enjoying her youthful beauty and kicking ass at her chosen career.

Then dickheads like Ken Andrews had to come along and make her feel like she was ready for a more serious, more exclusive (but maybe not 100% monogamous) relationship.

Absurd.

After a mentally stimulating panel about the current state of upscale office realty in New England, Lana and Roger made the rounds in the hotel lobby, the man much more interested in socializing than Lana was. Besides, Roger knew these people. He could do the heavy lifting in the socialization department.

Lana was busy, anyway. Busy grabbing for a glimpse of Ken whenever she could manage.

She saw him a few times. Usually she *felt* him before she saw his dashing vests or that perfectly groomed goatee on his face. Their eyes met more than once. *He asked me on a date tonight. I haven't given him my answer yet.* What a silly thing for her to do. She should have made up her mind that morning before they parted ways. Otherwise he was going to send her another $5 trinket and demand she meet him somewhere he owned. Like a bank. Or a hospital. Maybe an inner-city school.

Their eyes never met for more than half a second. This didn't bother Lana. What did bother her, however, was the flurry of butterfly wings kicking up trouble in her stomach every time that dark and seductive glance came her way. *Kill me. Right between the legs, you lecher.* Lana had to hold back the silly, girlish grin she wanted to have at that thought. She was in the middle of talking closing cost trends with a New Jersey agency.

"You know," an LA agent said, his SoCal tan bubbling beneath his rolled up Beverly Hills sleeves, "you have a look made for TV, Lana. I have it on good authority that one of the home improvement channels is going to start getting into real estate. Shows, that is. Casting calls popping up all over Hollywood. They're looking for agents, contractors, the whole works. But you can also bet they're going to care about looks first and foremost. Ever thought of being on TV?"

A Fated Night

Roger laughed; Lana paled. *Me? On TV?* People often said she had a Hollywood charm about her. It was the hair. Maybe the bold makeup. God knew she had a ball whenever she went to LA for work or pleasure. Living there, however, was not her style. She was a New England girl at heart. The Big Apple was her Big Picture, not the city of angels addicted to traffic jams.

"Lana really does have a face and figure for TV." Roger changed up the look he gave this Californian agent. *Don't tell me you want me to seriously consider this.* Or maybe Roger suddenly had a crush on this guy, not that he ever had good taste in anyone. *I bet Ken has good taste in men.* Lana had made sure to ask him more questions about those suggestions during their pillow talk time the night before. *He really would be too perfect if he was confident enough in his sexuality to occasionally fool around with men.* Confidence was sexy, but that level of confidence? Lana needed a new underwear collection to deal with the amount of arousal it foisted upon her. "You know, you must be the only west coast firm that's given us the time of day here."

The Californian laughed, gaze lingering on Roger's face. *Get a room, you two.* Lana would love it if her boss also got laid at this conference. That way if he ever found out about her and Ken he wouldn't have any room to give her shit.

"Lana has a reputation that currently precedes her," the agent said. "Everyone's talking about her." *I'm right here, for fuck's sake.* Typical men. *Talk about the lady as if she's not even here.* "We had dinner with the representatives with Lois & Bachman the other night and they had nothing but great things to say. You would have thought they knew you personally, Lana!"

"Lois & Bachman, huh?" She instinctively searched for Ken again, although he was nowhere to be seen. *I feel him, though.* It was a big lobby, packed with people coming and going to their rooms, checking in at the front desk, or conversing with the conference. There was currently one talk going on, but it was perhaps one of the least popular ones at the conference. Lana knew she wasn't going to it, anyway. "I didn't know I was *that* famous. Maybe I should go on TV after all."

Their cordial conversation came to an even more cordial end. As soon as Roger and Lana had a moment to themselves again, her boss launched with, "Lois & Bachman are talking about you, Lana. Do you know what that means?"

That I shouldn't have slept with their lead manager? Not that Lana regretted it. Ken was one of the best lays of the past few years. Certainly one of the best of her full adult life. *Sometimes I miss the naiveté of my high school and college years.* Many grown men had been a constant disappointment. They were supposed to be disappointments when she was in school. Now she wanted a real man who could satisfy her while still letting her be herself.

Having a few days of that with Ken was better than having a tenuous business relationship with him. He was right. Their attraction to each other was too strong to make for a good work environment. At some point they would have cracked and slept together. With Ken in a position of power over his new star agent? It was good of him to recognize that would have only spelled doom for Lana.

"No, Roger, tell me what that means."

A Fated Night

He *tsked* at her while simultaneously dragging her into a quiet corner. "Lois & Bachman," he began with a hushed voice, "are the biggest firm to hit New York in the past two years. I don't have to remind you of that, truly?"

"No, Roger, you sure don't."

"Didn't think so. They're your holy grail here, Lana. Get in bed with them. Not literally, of course. Like I said, Ken Andrews doesn't piss where he does business."

Men and their dick imagery. Well, he wasn't wrong. Ken had made it clear he was exactly like that, but he said it with better terminology. *He may have reaffirmed that while fucking me for the third time last night.* By the time they were done and ready to sleep, that bed was so torn up Lana would have never guessed they were in a nice suite at a historical hotel on Fifth Avenue. "I don't think they're the kind of agency I would fit in well with."

"What the hell? Are you crazy? You go big or you go *home* to rural Virginia in this business. You know that. Come on. Don't be stupid. Why would you even say something like that?"

She shrugged. "Call it my business intuition. I don't doubt they would do a lot of good for my career, but what about after I have to move on from them? Where do I go up from there?"

"I can't believe you're saying this bullshit." Roger sighed. "Oh, look, there are your new friends right now. David! Ken!" He waved down the representatives of Lois & Bachman on their way by. "You two remember Lana, right? *Don't blow this, Lana,*" he hissed in her ear.

Haha. Little did he know about her and blowing one half of the representation here.

"Yes," Ken said. He shook Lana's hand again as if they hadn't seen each other since they first met;. "Of course I remember the talented Ms. Losers. It's David here you should be asking that question." He winked at both Roger and Lana. David Bachman was oblivious and answering a phone call. "Or not. Never mind, then. I apologize on behalf of David. He really has no manners."

Roger chuckled. "Are you two busy tonight? We really should have dinner or at least drinks if you're available. I've been sent on a mission by *my* boss to get the scoop on New York. He wants to take our agency to the next level. If we could be half of what you are down in DC, I would die a rich and happy man."

"Then I'll be kicking myself for leaving your agency," Lana said. *You're so full of shit, Roger.* There were no plans to expand in that manner. Roger's boss made millions being the king of middle class real estate in the DC metro area, with only a few high-price tickets on the side. *Not enough to keep me happy.*

Ken gave them a shrug that suggested there was nothing he could do. "Unfortunately, we are booked solid for dinner. I've already promised someone else my... I mean *our* time." Lana was the only one who caught him giving her a spare look. *Right. Dinner.* Perhaps this time Lana would eat more around him than his cock. Speaking of, did he get his trousers from a tailor? Because they were doing very nice things to his crotch. *Calm down, you damn slut.* Lana needed a drink. Maybe more wine. She liked what happened when she drank wine near Ken.

"Terribly sorry to hear that. Perhaps tomorrow?"

A Fated Night

"I'll take a look at my planner when I have the chance. Excuse me, Mr. Prescott, Ms. Losers. I must collect David and take him to check in with *my* bosses." Before he left, he reached into his vest pocket and pulled out two business cards for them. He only looked at Lana long enough to be professionally kosher. "Perhaps I will see you later."

Now *that* got another glance in Lana's direction… and the quickest wink she had ever seen.

A part of her wished that he had been over her after one night together. Move on. Get back to business. *But I was the one who said I wanted a conference fling.* Lana wanted his cock inside her at least once a day until she had to go back to DC and the unfortunate dating pool there. She was under no delusion that their fling would last more than the length of the conference. She might as well get all she could out of this man.

"Hey, Roger," she said, turning on her sweet voice that made most men bend over to accommodate her. This included Roger, even though he would never admit it. "Can I borrow your laptop for a minute? I want to check my email."

"Oh for…" Roger reached into his bag and pulled out the heavy chunk of plastic that was his laptop case. "Fine. But only because I'm tired of carrying it around anyway." He had been using it to take notes at panels and presentations. Him and every other real estate Joe with the same great idea. Never before had Lana seen so many cords plugged into outlets, since at best a laptop like Roger's only got two hours of battery life. *We truly are in the technological age.* Lana barely knew how to use a laptop, so this was always a hoot.

She sat in the first available chair that had its back to a wall. The laptop was hot against her thighs, its fan already kicking up a fit the longer she kept her skirt pressed against the vents. *Shut up and let me do this.* Roger was already logged in. All she had to do was locate the browser, wherever it was. Whatever happened to Netscape, anyway? Oh! There it was!

"Don't change my homepage again," Roger warned her. "Last time you used it I opened up my laptop to find Google. Don't do that."

Just to spite him, Lana went to Google's homepage and may or may not have agreed to let it be the new permanent one. Besides, she had some searching to do before checking her email. *One of these days I'll get my own laptop.* She was holding off on buying an overheated clunker until she was at a new firm. Until then, she would use her desktop back home and be happy with it.

"Kenneth Andrews real estate," she typed into the search bar. After her date last night, she was hankering to learn more about the man who always had something else hidden up his tasteful sleeves.

Right away she was led to his personal profile page on the Lois & Bachman website. A professional headshot looked back at her. *Hello, Mr. Sexy.* Lana had to contain her excitement. She wasn't here to look at pictures of the man she made love to two nights in a row. She wanted deets. Lots and lots of delicious details.

He's not even thirty yet? Whoa. Lana had pegged him to be at least in his early 30s, if not a solid thirty-five. That had nothing to do with how he looked and everything to do with his position in his prestigious company. Plus, the amount of self-assurance that man carried was something she attributed to older men, not one still in his twenties. Not that his profile gave his birthday. It simply said he graduated with a Master's in Real Estate Development a mere few years ago.

When Lana scrolled through the other places he had worked for, she was less surprised to see how successful he now was. Some of the nicest firms (of various sizes) in New York had once hosted him as an intern or outright paid him to be their right-hand man. Lois & Bachman was a gig he entered as an agent and now controlled in lieu of the actual Lois & Bachman. *"Ken has been the lead manager of our firm since early 2002. He's ready to take a look at your needs and help you make the best plan of attack in today's market."* Lana also knew he owned at least one nice hotel and wanted to, oh dear, diversify into other areas of real estate holdings. If that wasn't sexy enough…

She then did a search on his family. Aha! No wonder. The Andrews were an old money family going back a hundred and fifty years. His father was one of the biggest investment bankers in Boston. No wonder Ken had started creating his own success at an early age. Lana was very familiar with how a little nepotism and a lot of family money could open important doors. *Still, we ain't as rich as these people.* Sexier and sexier.

Before Roger could peek at what she was doing, Lana opened her email and stared at the business card in her conference media packet. *kennethandrews@loisbachman.com* was about to get a flirtatious email from his lover of the moment.

Cynthia Dane

"Do you still want to meet for dinner? You and me? I'll leave Roger to rot for another night, although I'll have to think up a good reason. Any ideas? I've already pretended to be sick."

She fired off that email and wondered how she was going to ask to use this computer again later. Either that or she would have to pay to use the hotel computer later that evening, and that was gross. *I'd be better off going down to the Mac Store and finally treating myself.* She didn't doubt half the male contingency of the conference would volunteer to condescend to her about electronics.

To her shock, a reply popped up right away.

"Tell him you're meeting an old friend for drinks. Trust me, Bunny, your boss is peddling you like candy to schoolchildren at this conference. He doesn't actually need you *to sell you... hm, no wonder he's so successful at selling dumps in DC."*

Lana giggled. Dangit. Why did this guy make her *giggle?* It got Roger's attention, his cocked eyebrow silently asking if she needed some medicine for her extreme change in personality. Lana said something about a funny email forward and searched for Ken one last time. Oh, there he was. All the way on the other side of the lobby with his laptop in his lap, legs casually slung one over the other and his jacket off. *I could take off more of his clothes for him.* Lana didn't usually go for the businessman type, but Ken absolutely did it for her. He had to be one of the only men that made her fantasize about entering his office and crawling beneath his command center desk to give him the oral sex of his life.

"Like how he tried to barter me off to you a few minutes ago?"

A Fated Night

"*Like it? I'm not usually one who gets off on harboring secrets, but I get tingly thinking how nobody here knows about us.*"

"*You would be into that.*"

"*You aren't?*"

Lana sank so deeply into her chair that she almost couldn't peer above the laptop. Which was a shame, because no man was more worth looking at than Ken Andrews. "*I'm into a lot of things you don't even know about yet.*"

"*Tell me. Tonight at dinner. I know a great place around the corner from here. I'll have my assistant make reservations for us to dine in private. Then I'll take you back to my place so you can see one of the best views in Manhattan.*"

"*That better not be all I'm doing with those views.*"

"*Let's play it by ear. Meet me at Eden's at seven thirty. We'll treat it like a real date.*"

Lana considered the man making eyes at her from across the room. He did it so casually that she almost forgot there were other people in the crowded lobby. "*A real date, huh? You do realize that tomorrow is the last day of the conference, right? I'm going back to DC in two days.*"

"*We'll talk about it at dinner. I look forward to it, Bunny.*"

Ken closed his laptop and shoved it back into his bag. Legs uncrossed. Stature improved. Ken couldn't afford Lana one more look as he said something to David Bachman and left the lobby by himself. Such a busy man. A busy man making time for little ol' Lana.

"I know this is like the second night in a row I'm bailing on you," she said to Roger. "But an old college friend of mine is apparently in town and wants to get drinks at seven thirty. Can you bear to be without me?"

Her boss was so dramatically put out by her free spirit that he was compelled to groan in his chair. "If I say no, will you honor that?"

"Absolutely not." Lana grinned. "I really want to see this friend. You can manage without me until I get my award tomorrow."

"If you say so."

"I do." Lana logged out of her email and handed Roger his laptop back. He instantly cursed her for changing his homepage from Yahoo! to Google. He'd have to live with it. Like he'd have to live without Lana for one more night. For all she knew, it was her last night to be with Ken, and she planned on making the most of it. Perhaps to spite her career possibilities, but she would pretend otherwise.

Chapter 8

"It Doesn't Have To End, You Know."

There wasn't enough time to go shopping for a cute new date outfit, so Lana had to make due with one of the few outfits left in her luggage. When she was free from other responsibilities at seven, she hurried up to her room and changed into the first dress she grabbed. So happened it was a sexy and chic black cocktail number that she had planned on wearing to her award party the next night, but was willing to reserve for a man named Ken Andrews tonight.

Did he like her hair up or down? Should she go with a smoky eyeliner or ease up a bit? How far away was Eden's? She could wear her black stilettos, right? Oh, good, it was still light outside. Lana reused her black blazer from the night before but had every intention of taking it off when she met up with Ken.

Eden's was deceptively far away. Ken had told her it was around the corner, but in reality, it was a total of four blocks away: two south, two east. Long blocks, too! *Should've taken a cab.* It was already 7:40 by the time she made it.

"Hi," she said to the maître d' at his stoic podium. *Damn, this place is nice.* Softly lit, quiet, and radiating a scent of rose petals from every tealight candle. Lana had to wonder how Ken got reservations at the last minute. "I'm supposed to be meeting someone here. I'm a few minutes late."

"With whom are you dining, madam?" A bushy mustache tickled the man's nose as he looked over the reservations list.

A familiar touch caressed the small of her back. Lana was startled at first, but as soon as she realized it was Ken encircling his arm around her and speaking softly past her ear, she relaxed. The maître d', however, widened his eyes and flipped his reservation book shut. Suddenly Lana no longer existed. Only the possessive man making sure everyone in their vicinity knew she was his, if only for one or two more nights, mattered.

"She's with me, Charles." A hip-shaking kiss lightly touched her earlobe. "See to it that we're comfortable, please?"

"Yes, sir. Absolutely, sir." The maître d' leaped out from behind his podium, grabbing two menus from their stash on his way by. "Please, right this way."

"Wow." Lana nestled easily into Ken's hold. Only a few other diners glanced in their direction on their way by, but those who did were treated to a side of Lana she never got to express. What was it? What made her so giddy to be treated like this by a New Yorker? Was it the jealousy in the other women's eyes? The jealousy in the *men's* eyes? Because these two had shown up at the last minute, looking effortless together as they were escorted to one of the most private dining rooms in one of the most exclusive restaurants on the block?

It was a small room, but open enough to give them some breathing space as they sat down at the two-person table. Cinnamon red candles burned alongside a small centerpiece of daisies and baby's breath. Not the kind of flowers Lana expected at an upscale place like this, but she had no issue accepting the chair Ken pulled out for her.

"You really went all out." She shed the top of her blazer before her date's hands were on her, helping her remove the rest of it in one fluid motion. Ken draped it across the back of her chair. Lana experienced more than a few chills when she pushed forward without his aid. *Oh, look at that, this table is the perfect shelf for my boobs.* Good thing she had enough cleavage to make any man hard, let alone one as amicable as Ken. "I don't know *how* you got a reservation like this at the last minute."

He sat across from her. After ordering a bottle of Chardonnay from the maître d', Ken said, "You really can't think of a single reason I would be able to do this?"

No. No way. This was too much. "Don't you dare tell me that you own this place too."

"As it so happens, I acquired it about two months ago."

Lana dropped her menu before she had the chance to open it. "You're kidding! What else do you own?"

"I also own a couple of boutiques, but I'm thinking about offloading them to someone who can better watch over them.

Think I'll stick with hospitality and office buildings in the future."

"You're ridiculous." Lana looked over the menu. Dang. Most of the entrees were at least a hundred dollars. That didn't include drinks, appetizers, sides… if Lana got whatever she wanted, she would put this man (the owner, no less) out an easy few hundred dollars. Not that Ken Andrews, second son of one of the biggest investment bankers, couldn't afford it. "What's your long term plan, anyway? Do you work for someone else or do you work for yourself?"

"I believe in putting both to work for now." Ken only took one glance at the menu before shutting it again. "I recommend the salmon. Some of the best you'll get in this city."

"What do you mean by that? The first thing you said."

Ken offered to pour the Chardonnay when it arrived, leaving the poor maître d' with nothing else to do for now. Once he was dismissed, the drink began to flow, splashing beautifully into the crystal provided for their dining pleasure. "My job does bring in a sizable income, but I already have plenty of money in my investments. Ideally I see my job at Lois & Bachman as my ticket to networking. There's a reason I volunteered to come to this conference. I want to know as many people as possible before I go on my own."

"Your own agency? I remember you saying something about that last night." Their actual conversations were somewhat of a blur since all Lana could really remember was the endless fucking and nipple sucking. "You know, when your face wasn't crushed between my thighs."

A Fated Night

Ken's sizzling smile was only matched by the way he sipped his first taste of the Chardonnay. Lana waited until he put his glass back down before coyly plucking the stem and bringing the glass to her own lips. Why drink her glass when she could indirectly kiss him?

"I'm not sure exactly what I want to do yet. I don't really want my own agency, per se. Employees, yes, but not like what you and I are used to right now." He wavered between making love to her with his entrancing eyes and admiring the Chardonnay in his glass. Or perhaps he was taken with Lana's fingertips massaging his glass. Oh, that must've been it. Why else would he slip his fingers over hers and hold them there? Their thumbs circled in an endless, sweet flirtation. It made Ken clear his throat before continuing. "I want to build an empire that is all my own. Trouble is, that's hard to do without a partner, and I would need a partner I absolutely trust with that sort of enterprise. Hence the networking."

"Is this an immediate plan?"

"I'm hoping within the next few years. Once I've built up a sizable enough portfolio I can decide what's working and what I can learn from."

"Sounds interesting." Lana had often wondered how that worked. She knew plenty of bigshots who no longer ran agencies and instead bought and sold properties entirely for their own benefits. True, most of them worked with their families. Unless Ken's family members were all into real estate like he was, then there wasn't much point jumping in.

"Have you ever thought about striking out on your own?"

Lana sighed. This wasn't exactly what she had in mind for a date night. "Sometimes. I don't think I'm in a position where that's a viable fantasy, though. I've still got a lot to prove to others in the industry. Let alone to myself."

"That's wise. But you're young. Within twenty, thirty years I don't doubt you'll control a whole city somewhere."

"You're young too." Lana pulled her hand away. "I did a little digging into you, Mr. Andrews. I had no idea you were barely a year older than me."

"Is that all? I thought we were the same exact age."

"Hardly. You got a head start on me, though."

"Ah, I didn't think my age mattered. Although I would say I intentionally hide how young I am at times. Most people assume I'm older than I am, and I'm happy to let them do that."

Lana could see why. People probably took him more seriously in his position. "I wish you luck in your professional endeavors," she sincerely said. "Can we talk about something else now? It's a date night, right? We should talk frivolously about ourselves. I'm paying you for pleasure, Mr. Andrews."

He propped his chin up on his hand. *Keep looking at me like that and I'll have to kiss you.* She already planned to kiss him plenty that night. No sense jumping in right now. Maybe. "What are you paying me with, exactly? Because I don't recall any money changing hands. You don't know. Maybe all these buildings I own are in the hole and need a woman like you to save them."

"Sounds like a reverse rom com."

A Fated Night

"If I had to choose, I would rather live in a romantic comedy than a Sparks novel."

"Don't tell me you read Sparks."

"Who the hell has time to read? I watch the movies."

"Really." Lana could almost imagine it. Ken Andrews, sick in bed, flipping through channels and making the mistake thinking that *A Walk To Remember* was some feel good romance. Lana was forced to watch that movie with her little sister and spent the whole two hours wishing Mandy Moore would go back to singing songs about licking candy. That was more Lana's speed. "You watch tragic romance movies."

"I watch all kinds of movies. What's wrong with romance as a genre? I'd rather feel good about the human condition than watch another truck explode."

"Sheesh, I really don't get you." Lana was almost grateful that the waiter arrived to take their orders. She would take Ken's advice and get the salmon. "You're a total enigma."

"Then maybe you should take the time to get to know me better." Ken placed his order and kept his mouth shut until the waiter quietly excused himself. "Outside of the bedroom."

"That's what I'm saying. Let's talk about anything but work."

"Good." Ken leaned on the table, his left hand sliding across the fabric with graceful ease. Lana instinctively uncurled her fingers to take his in a light, cautious grip. "I'd like to get to know you too. Like you *did* say, it's a date." He lifted her hand and gently kissed her bent knuckles, a furtive gaze to light the ages on fire burning in his eyes.

When Lana packed her suitcase a few days ago, she never expected spending every night with a man like Ken. Hell, the only men she thought she would spend her evenings with were Roger and whatever guys he wanted to introduce her to. Being seduced – and doing some seducing on her own – her first night there wasn't exactly on her radar, although she hadn't been opposed to it. Seeing that same guy every night, even going so far as to accepting a *real* date from him and inevitably going to his place for sex? Maybe more? Ridiculous. Utterly ridiculous. Lana didn't do shit like that. Why? Because there were no men in the world worth doing shit like that with. One and done. Maybe more hookups here and there if they were worthy enough of her troublesome pussy.

Yet being with Ken in friendlier manners like these seemed so natural. He was easy to talk to. Willing to talk about himself while also asking Lana questions. Maybe he was the best fake listener in the world. At least he had Lana fooled after she went on a tangent about an embarrassing event in high school that garnered a laugh from him.

Almost seemed like a shame that they would have to go their separate ways in two days. But maybe, if Lana accepted a job at a New York firm… they could see each other again?

Ken was in the midst of talking about growing up with three brothers when he caught Lana staring into the distance. Their hands had never once detached through their dinners. The waiter had to contort his arms to set their dinners right in front of them. If Ken didn't care, Lana didn't either. This was his restaurant, after all.

A Fated Night

"What's wrong?"

She jerked her head back toward him. "Nothing. Thinking about what happens when I go back to DC."

Ken squeezed her fingers with one hand and rubbed his facial hair with the other. "What happens when you go back to DC?"

Oh, boy. "I go back to my life."

"Is it a good life, at least?"

"I suppose. It's... you know..." She wasn't blushing. Come on. Lana Losers didn't blush unless making a sale depended on it. *What am I selling right now?* Her body? Her mind? Her time?

"No. Enlighten me."

Lana needed more Chardonnay. Too bad they had almost downed the whole bottle while they were there. "I've had fun with you."

At first she didn't think he heard her. Then he squeezed her fingers even tighter, as if to reassure the insecurities festering in her stomach. The ones that said, *"This guy doesn't really want you. You're a fling. Treat him like a fling too. Don't get hurt because you were stupid."*

"It doesn't have to end, you know."

She was afraid he would say that. "I can't do long distance stuff. I get quite needy, really. If I went to DC and you stayed here, I'd be calling you every night to talk about nothing and demand phone sex."

"Well, you've convinced me. That sounds like a horrible life." Was he rolling his eyes? "Besides, I was under the impression that you wanted to move to New York for the next phase of your career. Just because you're not working for my company doesn't mean we couldn't see each other."

"Conflict of interest," Lana pointed out. "Depending on the firm, it could be considered me turning traitor."

"Why, Ms. Losers," Ken said. "If I didn't know any better, I'd think you were coming up with excuses for us to not keep seeing each other."

"I'm being practical." Honestly, Lana hadn't intended to get this quarrelsome, let alone about this subject. "It's not practical to date when we live hours apart. I'm guessing we work enough weekends that we would rarely see each other. How often do you come down to DC?"

"Not very often, I admit."

"Exactly, and I don't come up to New York all that much."

"Anything could change."

"I suppose."

"Bunny." That softly spoken name always made her heart do erratic things in her chest. *Who is he to call me something like that? My boyfriend? My husband? Yet I fall for it like some girl with her first love…* "Come back to the present, please. We'll worry about that nonsense later. Tonight is supposed to be fun."

She abashedly pushed aside her mostly-eaten dinner. "Would you want to keep seeing me after the conference is over?"

"You're the one who said this was a fling, not me."

I feel like some tides have been turned somewhere. Wasn't this supposed to be the other way around? Ken aloof about a more serious connection while Lana coyly begged him to take her on as his girlfriend? Oh, who was she kidding? He didn't want her to be his girlfriend. Maybe he thought he did, but Lana knew better than to believe something like that. It was almost too good to be true. In fact, she knew it was. No one was more cynical about the realities of love than Lana. She couldn't remember a single time in her life where she harbored those kinds of romantic fantasies.

Because she had always known they were impossible.

Her mother was the first one to break the news to her when she was a small child drawing up drama with her Barbies. *"How long until that Ken doll cheats on Barbie with that slut Midge?"* Juliet Losers spent half her time drunk. The only time she let up was when she was pregnant with her second daughter, not that her behavior improved much. *"No, wait, dickless Ken would want a brunette honey like Teresa. Calling it now."* Lana barely understood what her mother was talking about back then. One thing she could say, though? She had made it this far in her life and was never once cheated on. Her relationships never got serious enough for something like that to happen.

Thanks, Mom. Mothers. Always finding new and exciting ways to scar their daughters for life. Lana was glad she didn't want children. *I bet Ken* – and what an ironic name that seemed like now – *wants kids. A guy like him? Of course he does.* If he was as tender as he came off, then it was highly likely he wanted a small brood of little Andrews babies. He had a lot of brothers. Wouldn't he want a family like that too?

"I did say it was a fling. That's the only thing it could be, right?"

Ken's grip on her loosened. "If you say it's the only thing it could be, then it is. I won't argue with it."

"I'm sorry."

"Why are you sorry? You know what you want. Or don't want, in this case."

"I'm sorry because I got ahead of myself. You were right. Let's focus on tonight."

"Yes." Ken signed off on how much their dinner cost and gestured to the door. "Shall we?"

Lana sat up straight for the first time in forty-five minutes. *Yikes. My back.* Had it been worth it to hold that man's hand for so long? Lana was almost afraid to find out.

***

Goodness, did this woman ever really shut up?

Ken surprised himself with that thought, but Lana was a special case. It wasn't so much that she talked a lot. That didn't bother him. If he wanted to date a woman, then he wanted to hear her talk, right?

No, Lana's problem was that she talked herself into a pit of self-doubt. This wasn't the first time Ken saw it happen, and he figured it wouldn't be the last before they said their goodbyes at the end of the conference. *If she doesn't want a relationship, then why is she getting hung up on things?* Ah, maybe she wanted a relationship…

Ken had to admit that he was disappointed to hear her brush off the idea so brusquely. Sure, it would be difficult to

A Fated Night

date and further get to know each other living in separate cities, but Ken wasn't bothered by it. He always figured that the right woman would be worth any obstacles. The fact he put Lana in the contender class for *the right woman* after only knowing her for three days made this date even more important.

They held hands as they walked down Fifth Avenue toward Ken's apartment. Sure, it was possible that someone from the conference may be out and recognize them, but Ken didn't care. It wasn't a point of pride to be seen with a woman like Lana now. It was a point of ownership, of showing her off to other men who might be thinking about more than business with her.

"*See this woman here?*" he would say to any man from another agency. "*She's mine. You can hire her, but know that she comes home to me every night. That's right. Me. Do you want to mess with me? I didn't think so.*" His hand slipped out of hers and around her midsection. The closer he held her to him, the closer he felt their hearts beating in sync.

"We're here," he said with a quick kiss to her cheek. "Third location's the charm."

"The charm for what?" At least she was laughing again. A bubbly laugh like that deserved to be heard all the time. "Last I checked we had a pretty damn good record."

Ken nodded to his doorman, who held the front entrance open. "Oooh, you said one of my favorite words."

"What's that?"

"*Deed.*"

"You're a fiend."

"Why, thank you." Ken was glad to lead that grin into the executive elevator.

If Lana was impressed by his hotel and restaurant, he hoped she would be blown away by his Fifth Avenue apartment. While he didn't boast a penthouse – he didn't see much investment potential in that, currently – he did have a fantastic view, and the insulation was equally superb. Not a single one of his neighbors was ever going to hear what he got up to in his bedroom.

Sure enough, Lana darted straight from the entrance to his living room windows. The New York skyline had to look almost mythical to anyone not used to it. *Is she thinking this is the kind of place she wants to live? Is she so entranced she doesn't remember where she is?* Ken dumped his keys and wallet in a glass bowl by the front entrance. He then cautiously approached Lana, who was still wearing her blazer, and all those other unfortunate clothes too.

"This could be yours one day." He embraced her from behind, careful to not startle her while still fulfilling his desires to hold her close to him. Lana smelled of a large, hot, lavender bath that Ken was eager to climb into. *I am definitely climbing into her tonight.* Three times the night before was not enough. He had only been thwarted by biology. Otherwise, he would've kept fucking her until daylight came again. "I mean the view, that is. Play your cards right and you'll have a home like this."

"I thought my apartment back home was nice." Lana leaned back into his embrace, arms covering his. Her head rested on his shoulder. Ken soon forgot what his view looked

A Fated Night

like as he became too involved with the nape of her neck. He hoped Lana understood what he wanted. Now.

This woman was quickly becoming the end of him. No matter how controlled he was in the realm of the world, deep inside he was as convoluted and losing his senses as the base common man. From the moment he first shook Lana's hand, he knew there was something special about her. Something *otherworldly*. The first kiss completely destroyed him, even if he didn't know it at the time. While he had kissed many beautiful people before, Lana was her own brand of diabolical and delicious. He felt like he was kissing a queen.

No, a goddess.

Those other bastards wouldn't know how to treat her. Lana wasn't impressed by cock grabbing and money thrown at her. She could go out hunting for cock and make her own money whenever she wanted. So far, the things that seemed to impress her most were worshipping her for the deity she was while quietly proving his own net-worth. Because Lana had definitely been surprised (and impressed) by the properties he owned. Why? It wasn't because of the money he currently held. That couldn't be it. Perhaps there were some unknown goals lurking within that bright brain of hers.

Yes, yes, good for her. She's witty and intelligent. Ken was reaching the point of this date where he didn't care if Lana could sing an opera solo or solve complicated math equations. He cared that her curves nestled perfectly against his body and that her breath was caught in her throat every time he caressed her.

"Fuck me," she muttered. Excellent. Similar thoughts.

"In a moment." Ken removed his jacket and tossed it over the back of a chair. Lana stood in the middle of the room, taking in his dark, masculine décor and the minimalist furniture inviting her to sit down. Ken liked to think he had an eye for design, but rarely had the time to indulge in it. Instead, he hired interior designers who had the same exact taste as him and rarely needed consulting. The latest one had nailed what he envisioned for this place. Did Lana like it? Why did he care? *Imagine me and you, Ms. Bunny, buying properties like this and turning them into something amazing.*

Whoa.

Where did that thought come from?

Lana turned, a wide, quizzical look meeting Ken from across the room. She was so... vulnerable. The thoughts swarming her mind were right there broadcasted on her face. Too bad Ken was still mostly illiterate when it came to reading her thoughts. *I want to learn to read her.* He wanted to know what that turn of her head meant. What that look relayed. What the slight change in the tone of her voice and the sharp intake of breath conveyed. It wasn't enough getting to know her sexual responses. Ken wanted to read her soul through those pretty, sparkling eyes.

To be the only man who could claim such a feat? That was worth more than his whole fortune put together.

Fuck. Me. Ken kept his visage pristine while facing her. He would not let Lana see the turmoil festering in his heart.

He had never really known what love was. He thought he had. Even thought he had loved a few women through the

A Fated Night

years, before being proven wrong. No. No, here it was. Love was embodied in a woman who was too superb to be real. Too headstrong to be his inferior in any way. Too cunning to be overpowered in whatever industry she tackled.

Too impossible to realistically have. She said so herself. This was a fling. Ken needed to steel his heart from any possible break coming for it. Lana Losers was the epitome of heartbreaker if she put that amazing mind to it.

I want her. Ken took a few steps toward her, hoping she would meet him in the middle. *I want to rule the world with her.* Was that too much to ask? To take her hand and draw her into a kingdom of their own ruling? *I want to be completely one with her.* That was the love talking. The pure, unadulterated emotion that made life both so frightening and yet so worth living.

"Do you believe in fate?" he asked Lana.

Lana slowly shook her head. "I don't like the idea that I'm not in control of my destiny."

He was close enough to hold the back of her head with a steady hand. Her golden hair covered his hand with a softness that had touched his skin before, but never his heart. *Damn you, Lana Losers. I wasn't ready for this.* He was going to pursue the full extent of his career before pursuing a romantic partner. Why did this have to happen now? With a woman who thought distance was too much to bear? No, no, that wasn't the only thing closing Lana off romantically. She had no reason to believe in what Ken currently felt.

"Sometimes it's good to give up control." Ken wiped a small remnant of dinner away from the corner of her mouth –

an excuse to touch that smooth cheek. "I don't mind giving up control now and then."

That had spoken to something deep inside of her. *I know how she reacted when I implied I'm up for almost anything.* The only thing that had turned Lana on more than the thought of him with a man for her enjoyment was the thought of dominating him. Well, shit. If there were ever a woman in the world who should get the honor...

Except that wasn't what she needed right now. She needed to let go, to open her heart to him and to experience what it meant to completely embrace the joys of a sexual connection.

"I've never done it like that before."

"Like what?"

Lana placed her hand upon his. *Don't make me stop touching you.* She didn't. "Like what you're talking about. I've only given myself over like that in a purely sexual way."

Ken wasn't surprised. The only times a woman like Lana would open her heart in bed was if it was vanilla to a fault. The kinkier things got, the more it was about her sexuality and nothing more. No issue with that. Ken saw lots of benefits to approaching one's single sex life like that.

Didn't really work in an actual relationship. That's what he desperately wanted right now. More than he wanted to conquer half of Fifth Avenue with stealthy acquisitions nobody knew he had the means of accomplishing.

"Let me in?"

Lana kept her stance rigid, but inside she crumbled. A gleam in her narrowing eyes. A bite of the lip. Reddening ears.

A Fated Night

Drooping curl on the side of her forehead. Had Ken asked the impossible? Of course he had. How could he be so stupid? He had to find a way to diffuse the spark he inadvertently lit.

"When you look at me," he said, easing his hold on the back of her head, "what is the first thing you think? Sexually speaking."

Strip away the emotions. Give her a blank slate. Make her think of things that were sure to improve her mood. Lana was not going to walk out of Ken's apartment with anything foul on her mind. That wasn't allowed.

Thank God she smiled. "You really wanna know?"

"I wouldn't have asked if I wasn't prepared for the answer."

That bite of her lip intensified. "I think about how I can show the world that I'm currently the mistress of your universe."

Well. That was... hot. Ken's cock definitely preferred this kind of talk to thoughts of falling in love and all the drama that came with it. "How would you do that?"

Hands fueled with purpose traveled up his chest. *She's devouring me, isn't she?* So happened that's exactly what Ken Andrews wanted. "I'd take you somewhere I could fuck you in front of everyone."

"Go on."

"I like to show off."

He tipped her chin up, enjoying the curve of her neck. "So do I."

"Stop being so perfect." Lana brought her lips to his but didn't go for the full kiss. She did, however, tug on his necktie, loosening it when she wasn't making it choke him. "You don't actually want to hear about my exhibitionist fantasies."

"I do if there's a possibility of them coming true."

"So you want to hear about me riding your cock while making eye contact with every onlooker in the room?"

Apparently. Or so his cock claimed when it hardened in record time. "Absolutely."

She glanced down between them. "I'll take both of your guys' words on it."

"You know what I'm really thinking about right now?" He caressed her collarbone, eager to kiss it – while completely sheathed in her cunt. *My bed is right over there.* So was his trunk of goodies he kept at the foot of the bed. Lots and lots of wonderful things hiding in there. He had a feeling Lana would be into it.

"No." Lana wrapped her arms around him. "Tell me. Then let's do it."

He'd see about that. "I'm envisioning you on my bed."

"Yes?"

"Naked."

"Ooh, yes."

Here was the kicker. "Blindfolded. Tied up." He pulled her closer, his erection bumping into her. "Completely at my whim to do with as I please, with any part of my body."

Ken feared she would withdraw from him. But when she remained resolute in his arms, he had a good feeling. That feeling only got better when she grinned at him. Every pearly white tooth enticed him to bite her in turn.

A Fated Night

"With you?" she said. "Sounds wonderful."

They sealed that mutual thought with a heart-pounding kiss.

Chapter 9

"Does Any Of It Bother You?"

Lana was alone in Ken's bedroom, taking in the private chambers of a man she was becoming way, way too attached to.

She was pretty sure he was attached to her too.

Don't think about that. She smoothed down her dress and fluffed her hair. Somewhere, Ken was probably watching her. *"Before you agree to anything,"* he had said shortly before going into his office for a few minutes, *"take a look in my trunk in my bedroom. It's unlocked."*

She stood in front of it now, dithering.

Oh, she knew what was in there. What else would a man keep in a large trunk at the foot of his bed besides kinky implements? The only thing keeping her from popping that lid open was the fact they were meant for her.

A Fated Night

Yesterday would've been a great time to unleash whips and chains. Maybe nothing crazy, since they had barely known each other, but Ken was someone Lana could see herself enjoying the finer pleasures of BDSM with. Finding out that he had a taste for it did not surprise her, nor did it dissuade her from wanting to explore that side of herself with him. *Would rather tie him up right now.* Beggars wouldn't be choosers.

"All right." Lana knelt before the trunk and located the two main latches. "Let's see what you've got, Mr. Andrews."

She expected every last thing she uncovered, yet she was still in awe over how meticulously arranged everything was. The top removable rack boasted different types of restraints, from handcuffs to malleable leather straps, each one carefully wrapped unto itself and then arranged in a tight, circular pattern. Beneath the rack were the spanking instruments arranged by Ken's personal pain scale: elegant feather dusters on the left, pockmarked paddles on the right.

It got more interesting from there. Ball gags. Leather and metal bondage gear. Glass and metal nipple clamps. Anal beads still in factory sealed packaging. Plugs that were plain and plugs that were clearly meant for prostate stimulation. G-spot stroking dildos and vibrators that packed a battery-operated punch. A small, detachable section of the lid revealed various kinds of lube and temperature controlled condoms. Most of them were the same size even if they were made of different materials… but there were a few smaller and a few bigger.

What kind of parties does this guy have? Lana wanted to attend one. Or all of them.

Then again, the perfect condition of everything – not to mention how neatly it was arranged – suggested that they were almost never used. Either that or Ken was so keen on letting his partners have new, hygienic materials to play with that he was constantly replacing his items.

"Anything speak to you in there?"

She heard him, but she did not turn to him. "Many old friends and new." She put everything back where she found it. Before she closed the lid, however, she withdrew a pair of black silk ropes and laid them neatly on top of the trunk. "You have quite the collection."

"I always try to be prepared. Never know what someone may beg for in the middle of sex." His tone implied that such a someone was Lana. *Well, I did demand that he spank me last night.* A lot. She was so red at one point that she could barely roll on her ass while getting from one end of the bed to the other. "Does any of it bother you?"

That wasn't insecurity speaking on his behalf. It was 100% polite curiosity. "Everything speaks to me to some extent." She stood. "Mostly good things."

"I spent ten minutes agonizing that I had gone too far."

Lana scoffed. "You'll have to try a lot harder to scare me off. I once dabbled as a professional dominatrix when I was a senior in undergrad." She had made good money during that short stint, too. Lana was told she was a natural. She could've made a solid career out of it. *Unfortunately, the real estate world called to me.* Too bad. All those men who missed out on Mistress Lana. She probably could have changed their lives.

A Fated Night

"I missed it?"

"Yes." Lana picked up one of the ropes and looped it loosely around Ken's neck. It draped down his shoulder like the front of a cape. "And I don't know what you would have been agonizing about. I was about to strip and wait for you on your bed. Naked." She wondered what his bed smelled like. Ken times infinity? Or was he the type to have his sheets washed every day so they always smelled like fresh linens? *Guess I'll find out pretty soon.*

"No, no…" Ken ignored the rope hanging on him as he guided Lana toward the bed. "I would've been disappointed." He hugged her close from behind. An erection as hard as the purr in his throat rubbed against her ass. "I want to take off your clothes myself."

"You're certainly more than welcomed to." Lana's hands landed on the bed. Ken's own hands immediately began to grope her, starting with the underside of her breasts and ending with two hearty squeezes to her hips. "As long as I get naked soon."

"Naked, tied up, and ready for mounting."

Lana shivered. "You can mount me anytime, mister."

He lightly spanked her ass before yanking up her skirt. A zipper descended, followed by five determined fingers raking her bare back.

"You're like unwrapping the greatest gift on Christmas morning." The dress tugged down Lana's body until she stood in nothing but her nudity and the black, sexy thong she wore for this occasion. The only agonizing part was having her nipples drag across the bed whenever Ken decided to move her a single inch. *At this rate I'm going to lose my mind and turn into some total nutjob slut who only sustains herself by banging dick.* Wow, when she put it that way, it didn't sound like a terrible thing at all! "I should get a bow to put on your head for my amusement. What do you think, my little bunny?"

She claimed a kiss to the lips. "I think you should do whatever you want, Mr. Andrews."

"Oh, I will."

The man had promised to do unspeakably amazing things to her. Lana was inclined to believe it could happen. Easily. Ken Andrews did not go back on his words. He had given her no reason to believe he would fool her with promises of ecstasy and then yank them away. Lana had only known the man for a few days, yet here they were, in his apartment overlooking one of the most expensive streets in America.

Ready to indulge in one of her favorite things.

He was gentle. Gentle in that his intentions were firm, but the hands wandering her naked body only had her pleasure in mind. Ken wasn't going to use her. He wasn't going to make her feel dirty – unless she begged for it. Even the way he lazily rolled her onto her back and hovered over her, still dressed in his business clothes while she was naked enough to feel her nipples peak, spoke of nothing but tenderness.

"You need a safe word," Ken said. "You choose."

While she thought about it, he kissed her skin all over, starting with her collar bone and meandering across her breasts. Lana sighed, happier than she had been in a long time... and ready to embrace this kind of happiness. "Bachman." It was the first thing that came to her mind, and *shouldn't* be popping up in her love life.

Ken nipped her areola. Shocks and shivers exploded from within. Moaning, Lana wrapped her arm around him and drew him down for a harder kiss. He circled her navel in warning before sliding his hand between her legs and over her mound.

"You're wet," he observed.

"You make me wet."

One finger penetrated her, testing how wet she was. "Uh huh…" When his finger pulled back out, it grazed her clit, sending furious arousal on the prowl through every inch of Lana's body. "I'll let you in on a little secret: a man being able to get a woman wet like this is considered a pretty fantastic compliment. But you knew that, didn't you?"

"I may have had an idea."

He fingered her for a few more seconds before getting up again. Lana rolled over, despondent to be so alone again – but not afraid of it. Ken would come back. She had been promised unspeakable things, after all.

The ropes she had picked out landed on the bed. Ken removed his vest and unbuttoned the front of his shirt. "Drink it in, lovely lady." He loosened his necktie. It slipped off him easily. "My body's the last thing you're going to see for a while."

***

Lana had been tied up and blindfolded more times than she cared to try to count. However, all of those encounters came in two flavors, neither of which she and Ken espoused as a certifiable truth. Either those men (and wasn't there one woman in there?) were partners she had known for a while, or were professionals she met for the sole purpose of having a physically good time. Sometimes she even paid for the experience, such as a birthday present to herself or because she was having a rough few weeks. She had never, *ever* gone this far this quickly with a man she was kinda-sorta seeing and only had a vague idea of what his history was. For all she knew, he was an incompetent buffoon who, at best, would blunder his way uncomfortably through this experience. At worst? Lana didn't want to think about that.

Ken was so easy to be around. From the moment he put a hand on her, she was ready to go and eager to trust him. *Yes, yes, I want to have this kind of experience tonight.* Maybe this was the moment he turned into a crazy serial killer. Lana was willing to take that chance.

Well, she was committed now, and wasn't inclined to believe that she had much to fear, for even though her wrists were bound above her head and her calves pressed against her thighs, Lana Losers was so far removed from fear that she couldn't imagine doing anything but trust the brilliant man kneeling between her legs and licking her slit with a mixture of grunts and growls.

While Lana assumed this gift was mostly to make sure she was wetter than wet for what was to come, she also liked to

A Fated Night

believe that Ken was having the time of his life down there. Then again, Lana was unfortunately familiar with men who would rather eat haggis than go down on a woman, but gave it the ol' college try anyway. *Worse than what fake lesbian porn looks like, honestly.* Ken was nowhere near that kind of embarrassment. His tongue sensually licked her cleft, diving deep, deep, *deeper* into her than she thought possible for a man to accomplish. The eagerness he foisted upon her mound was only matched by her swelling clit and the wet arousal leaving her body faster than she could control it – as if such things could be controlled. *He must think I taste good.* And felt good, since there was no way to fake the way he clutched her thighs, massaged her stomach, and flirtatiously licked the entire length of her slit. The man was feasting. Lana was the most delectable meal he had ever consumed.

She was not gagged, but she was under a silent order to not speak. Ken was in control; she submitted to him. Not easy for Lana to submit under most circumstances, even when it was what she wanted. It required opening a special part of her heart and soul that often didn't see the daylight. *I have to be vulnerable. I have to trust the person doing this.* Sometimes fear seized her. It was easy to forget how many times Ken had been kind to her already. Kindness was in short supply when it came to competent lovers.

Although she couldn't see him, she knew what he looked like based on the sounds, the sensations, the knowledge she already had of what it was like to be with him. *His hair is already mussed from rubbing against my thighs… every time he turns his head and rubs his prickly face against my cunt.* She loved it. That feeling. The intimacy it bestowed between them. *His eyes are closed. He has no reason to look me in the eye when I'm blindfolded, so he's completely savoring every second that goes by. His mouth is pursed from all the sucking and licking. I can't avoid seeing it. I know that's what is happening.* Ken Andrews was drunk on her pussy. Her wetness was all over his face and in his hair. The man would need a thorough shower to get her off him. Hopefully not for a while.

Of course it felt good. Of *course* she wanted to cry out, moan, thrust against his face and encourage him to bring her to orgasm. But Lana knew that this wasn't about that. Ken was proving himself to her, one heavy lap of the tongue at a time.

Then he really went for it. Got right in her center, hands bracing against the undersides of her thighs and demanding she give up an orgasm to soothe his masculine ego that wanted to prove it could give it to her unlike any other man.

His tongue fucked her with purpose. His lips sucked, sucked, *sucked* so hard on her clit that Lana began to writhe from how intensely it shook her. The first real moan eked from her chapped lips. *Kiss me, baby. Come up and kiss me with that nasty mouth of yours.*

Instead, he used that mouth to make her come. He didn't even have to use his fingers. Just the judicious application of oral skills a man could only amass after a *lot* of practice.

Orgasm built in her stomach, right where his forehead touched her. It was like a button waiting to be pushed, to send off a flurry of fireworks through her whole body. Relax her. Claim her. Fuck her up until she couldn't move or speak any

A Fated Night

longer. The man had only penetrated her with one finger and his tongue, and yet she dared to think she could feel like that after an orgasm? She must have been insane.

Or really, really hopeful.

"Fuck!" She hadn't meant to say a word when she climaxed, but she couldn't help it. Ken kept going, eating her alive, destroying the last of the barriers erected between them. He was going to make her lose her mind, and she would beg to have it done again and again. "I'm coming!" Like she had to tell him. The man was already so attuned to her body's machinations that he had to know she was coming all over his face.

Bless a man who lived for that shit. Because Lana had a lot to offer him from the core of her body.

Endorphins tranquilized her almost instantly. *Don't need any tranquilizing, but shit, this is great stuff.* Lana completely gave herself over to every whim he had, every inclination she fostered in the bottom of her heart.

She smelled her scent before his lips touched hers. The familiar crinkles of a condom unwrapping enslaved her senses. Ken kissed her. His erection, freed from his pants at some point or another, pressed against her slick entrance. Still unsheathed. *Oh, God, that feels so good.* Lana was intoxicated on sex enough to think going bareback was the best idea ever. Yet if Ken was already getting out a condom, she wouldn't say no. *This is a fling, right? Be safe, dumbass.*

But the endorphins said a lot of things. Like how this wasn't a fling anymore.

She couldn't listen to them. Ken was kissing her, sharing her scent and taste with her. His tongue owned her mouth like it had owned her cunt. As soon as the condom was on, he pushed his cock a single inch into her, his sigh of relief breaking Lana in two.

Lana was forbidden from moving. The best she could do was raise her hips to meet his thrusts and turn her head this way and that. She didn't want to. She wanted to kiss Ken, fully and deeply, while he gently rocked into her at such a good angle. By the time he was completely in her, Lana was already sated from head to toe – but especially deep within. If anything, the best part of this kind of sex was acknowledging how easily her tight confines adjusted to accept him into her body. It was as if every part of her approved of him and the way he could make love.

"What do you want?" Ken whispered against her ear, his breath almost as hot as the sharp intakes diving down his throat. "Tell me what you want, and I'll give it to you."

Lana wanted to be untied so she could wrap her arms around him while they had sex. But she also had no problems understanding what was so good about having her wrists bound above her head. *I am putting every ounce of trust I have into him. Just like every part of him is in me right now.*

"I want you."

Maybe it was her. Maybe it was some last, lingering naiveté she didn't know she still had. Maybe it was that, yeah. That was what made her think he *really* gave her all of him. His heart was on his sleeve, even though Lana couldn't see it. She could feel it beating, though. Bump. Bump. *Bump.* Just like the headboard thumping quietly against the bedroom wall. Ken gave her strong, thorough thrusts that brought every delicious inch of his cock closer to her core. *Hell yes.* He didn't have to fuck her brains out to give her the perfect experience. It was good enough that Lana was tied up for him, bare, brazen, beautiful. *I feel beautiful. I feel like the most desirable woman in the world.* That was how Ken treated her when he wasn't preoccupied with kissing her, his hands sometimes on her cheeks, but mostly touching her bare skin all over.

"I want you too," he said a minute later. How long had he been thinking that? "Fuck me, you don't know what you do."

She had a good idea now. But again, that could've been the last remnants of her naiveté making her feel like a girl again.

She could be a princess.

She could be a *queen.*

All she needed was the perfect Prince Charming who understood her inside and out. Who didn't question who she was or what she liked in bed and out. Who wouldn't be threatened when she commented on someone else's attractiveness or even dared to suggest they *see where this goes.* Who would foster crazy levels of delusion for fun and games when the time was right. Who would bring her back down to reality when it was demanded of them. But who would do so with such a gentlemanly quality that Lana didn't even notice it.

She didn't realize until then, when Ken upped his thrusts and his cock became almost unbearably large, that she really did have a type of man. Turned out it was a man like Ken.

That's so stupid. Lana didn't want to get lost in thoughts like this. She wanted to run away from them, to embrace the sexual euphoria getting ready to explode in the both of them. Ken was about to come. His voice was caught in his throat, breath blasting against Lana's skin. Whimpers. Moans. Groans. Grunts. She didn't know which sound belonged to whom. She *did* know what was the mattress squeaking and the headboard hitting the wall, but that didn't tell her who growled in imminent orgasm and who whimpered to be on the other end of it. Her inner walls contracted; his cock pulled his seed from his sack and brought him to that treacherous edge. *That's so stupid… I don't know this man. I don't know him. We've barely met. We've fucked. Maybe there's something wrong with the both of us. We don't even live in the same city. It would never work. Somebody save me.*

Ken was the only one who answered that call. Assuming "save me" meant fucking her until her thighs ached and she felt completely, utterly beneath his benevolent control.

"I'm coming, Bunny," he muttered into the crook of her neck. "Oh, fuck, I'm coming for you."

For her. Not for himself. Not for his ego. For her?

Lana came too, not a second after the first instance of orgasm took Ken down

Climax was long and drawn out for them both. Lana never reached the cataclysmic crest that would knock her out for hours. She wanted to experience every second with Ken, who cradled her in his arms and rocked his orgasm within her.

Out of all the things Lana could think about right then, realizing that she had never felt such an emotional connection

A Fated Night

during sex was not something she even considered before coming to New York. Wouldn't she know it? Within three days of touching down at JFK she was tied up in some man's bed, wondering if he was in love with her.

Not if she was in love with him. If *he* was in love with *her*.

That was how Lana deflected from her own issues. She couldn't face that question coming from her heart, only the one simmering in her mind.

It was the only way she could continue to enjoy her night.

"Wow," he said, still inside her, still on top of her. Lana's arms tired. Her thighs ached in both desire and fatigue. While she didn't want this to end, she knew her physical limits were going to make her do more than wish him off her. "You're one of the most amazing women I've ever been with."

She didn't doubt him. She was queen of her world.

"Bachman," she whimpered.

Ken was off her much sooner than she anticipated. "I'm sorry," he said. Was he back to his senses? That fast? "Here. I'll untie you."

Lana shook out her arms as soon as they were freed. Her toes wiggled when her legs stretched again. The two black ropes disappeared over the edge of Ken's bed. She sat up, knees pressed against her chest and arms wrapped tightly around her legs. Hair fell between her and Ken. He tucked some of it behind her ear. Lana leaned her cheek into his palm.

"Did I do something wrong?"

He was disheveled yet unbearably put together. Hair as mussed as Lana anticipated. Clothes wrinkled and speckled with her wetness. Watch hanging upside down on his wrist. Cock in need of freedom from a choking condom. Face coated in concern.

"No." Her knuckles caressed his goatee. "I was getting sore, that's all."

Their mutual gaze held until Lana had to push more hair out of her face. Ken kissed her hand and massaged the inside of her thigh. Not sexually, either. His fingers stayed a respectful distance from her folds.

"Why did you throw the ropes aside?" Lana could mess with him tonight too. "What makes you think I'm done with you, Mr. Andrews?"

His eyes widened in curiosity. "Give me a moment to get hard again, Ms. Losers."

"Who told you to get hard right now? Fuck that. A woman like me likes a little challenge. I guarantee I'll have you hard again in five minutes if you give me one of those ropes and take off the rest of your clothes." She winked at him. "You're not the only one around here who knows how to tie a knot and make someone feel vulnerable."

Ken gave her the exact reaction she wanted. He plopped down onto his bed, chin propped on his hand and smirk tearing her apart inside.

Her move.

***

A Fated Night

The hot, almost scalding water washing down Ken's skin was exactly what he needed after a night like the one he experienced. From the moment he woke up still tangled with Lana, he craved a good shower. So he skillfully pulled away from her, careful to not disturb her fitful sleep, and stole into his master bath for a well-earned rinse.

He needed a few minutes to himself anyway. Some minutes to sort through his thoughts and feelings that Lana had yanked out of his heart and put on display right before his very eyes.

The woman was beyond anyone he had ever been with, that was for sure. Ken had never met a woman who could seamlessly go from submitting to him like that to driving him wild with a silk rope. He didn't have to think too hard before memories of that silk against his cock and her lips gently sucking his tip reentered his mind. So much for morning wood being anything but sexual arousal.

He lathered himself with sandalwood body wash. *Such a stereotypical scent to get, isn't it?* Yet Lana hadn't complained. She was happy to bury her nose in his scent and smile serenely, as if that was the only scent she wanted to experience for the rest of her life. *You can, you know.* Ken would never say it out loud. That he wanted Lana for much, much longer than this conference would last.

Today was the last day. Tomorrow, Lana was going back to DC and whatever life she had there.

Honestly, how unfair. Why did she get to leave Ken to pick up whatever pieces were left in her wake? *So much for that fling she was talking about.* He was going to lose his mind at this rate.

Feel it explode in his skull and leave disgusting pieces all over his shower floor. With any luck, the shower water would wipe the tiles clean before the cleaning lady showed up to scream over what she discovered.

He didn't want to say he was in love. That wasn't fair to Lana or himself.

Ken washed the last of the shampoo and soap off his body. He was about to shut off the shower when a naked figure strolled into his bathroom, a picture of feminine veracity on the other side of his opaque shower door.

"Room for one more?" Lana leaned against the wall next to the shower entrance. Her sleepy look made Ken smile. Her naked, curvy body made that morning wood refuse to go away. "I need a shower too, Mr. Andrews."

He cracked open the door. "There's always room for you in here, Ms. Losers."

"Ooh, nifty." She pushed it open wide enough to step through. "You haven't seen anything until you see water dripping off these tits."

"You know how to sell a co-ed shower." Naturally, Ken's eyes went straight to her breasts once she stepped beneath the showerhead. He refrained from helping himself to them.

"So." Lana pulled her hair aside, letting the water spill over her shoulder and, yes, down her breasts. *Ah, yes, the ever-helpful nipple. So taut. So hard. So without my mouth on them.* What a crime. Mornings weren't supposed to be this hard. *Hm, nice choice of words, Ken...* "Today's the last day of the conference. Every heterosexual male there wants to bone me, and yet you're the only one who has had the honors. You're also the only one who doesn't want to hire me for his firm... heh, firm." Good to know that they both had dirty minds. "Where does that leave us, exactly?"

Dare Ken hope? "You were the one who called this a fling." He pulled his body wash off the shelf and gestured lathering her up. Lana shrugged with a smile on her makeup-less face. "I'm the one offering to make something work if you're willing to put in your half of the effort." He said that as soothingly as possible, or at least as soothingly as the pounding water against tile would let him. Ken assumed that his careful touch to her shoulders and hips as he worked the soap into a lather would be enough to get his intentions across.

"I know. You've said as much a few times." She lifted her hair so he could reach over her shoulders and grab her breasts. "Like I said, I don't do long distance relationships that well."

"You make it sound like we would be apart for months at a time. Hardly. It's not difficult to fly down to DC on weekends or fly you up. Or we could meet somewhere in between. I hear Boston is a lovely place for disgustingly sweet hookups."

She rested her head on his shoulder. Shower water blasted her chest, steam rising around their faces. "I'll think about it," she said. "Maybe you could further convince me tonight. I have to go to that party in my honor, but after that I fully expect to have someone give me my real reward for being the best realtor this past year."

"Oh, oh, pick me." He licked the water off her neck while giving her breasts a hearty squeeze. His cock tickled the length of her ass. Lana squirmed in giggling delight. "I know a lot of ways to congratulate you."

She turned in his arms, easing him against the shower wall. Hands explored his chest, his abs, the mess of freshly washed black hairs that surrounded his cock. His *hard* cock, he had to note. "Do you? You can get started now. I'm not leaving this shower without an orgasm to start my day."

Her hair was plastered against her skin now. Even drenched from head to toe, she was startling gorgeous… and apparently full of all sorts of ideas, for instead of asking him to finger her, to fuck her, or to eat her out one last time, she stroked the underside of his cock and slowly sank to her knees.

"But let's start with yours."

Ken would love to start every day of the rest of his life like this. What man wouldn't?

A Fated Night

Chapter 10

"She'll Be A Distraction."

"There you are!" Charlie Bachman approached with son David only a step behind him. Ken jerked up from his seat in the hotel lobby. Around his feet were the bags of conference materials he was putting together for Lois & Bachman's perusal on Monday morning. "Why the hell aren't you answering my calls, Andrews?"

What the hell is he doing here? Ken stood and instantly extended his hand for his boss to shake. Charlie continued to smile at him while shaking his hand, so apparently Ken was not in trouble. For now. "What calls?" He pulled his hand back and dusted off his pant leg. *I didn't realize until I left my apartment that I put on the wrong pants.* Most people wouldn't notice. Lana, who had followed a few paces behind him to the conference so she wouldn't draw too much suspicion, informed him via email that his ass looked oh so tight in those even tighter pants. "I never received any calls from you."

A perplexed Charlie parroted a phone number that no longer belonged to Ken. Not since he changed carriers and upgraded his phone two months ago. Sheesh. How could Charlie still be trying to use Ken's old number? Who had received a bunch of texts and voicemails regarding some stuffy real estate conference?

"I knew it wasn't right for you to ignore me like that." Charlie sat in the chair next to Ken's. His portly figure spoke of a man who had lived well his whole life. Technically, he and business partner Richard Lois had built their real estate enterprise from the ground up, but both men had extensive family connections and their own personal coin to get a head start on things. Ken wouldn't hold that against them, though. He couldn't. Otherwise he would be a hypocrite, and almost nothing disgusted him more. "I told myself that you were either so busy your world was crumbling at this conference, or that you had a lobotomy between the office and the hotel. Either way, figured I'd drop by and talk to you face to face."

"How good of you." Because what Ken really needed right now was the boss checking up on him. "I can assure you that everything has been going swimmingly." He wasn't talking about his love life, either. When Ken wasn't obsessing over Lana, he managed to get a fair amount of work done. Although, as the days went on, it became increasingly more difficult to ignore the pull drawing him and Lana together.

"How's the networking?"

A Fated Night

"Better than ever." Ken cocked one leg over the other so his largest binder balanced in his lap. Facts and figures from the most recent talk he attended still waited to be analyzed. Usually a man like Ken would have an assistant go over the figures in his stead, but if Ken wanted to run his own business one day, he needed to know every number intimately. Just like he knew Lana Losers intimately by now. "We've had private conferences with both the Miami group and the LA firm. There's a Philadelphia agency that proves to be a promising lead for future partnerships. Not to mention a rumor that Kevin, Schumer, and Lovitz from Providence might be in the market to sell." Keven and Schumer had been gravely injured in separate skiing accidents. Lovitz couldn't run the firm by himself so, Ken figured, there was an opportunity to sweep in and save the business while also moving into a lucrative business market.

Charlie waved these thoughts away with a wrinkled hand. "All good. Now, tell me about this woman everyone is gossiping like they're in a hen house about."

The pen flicking between Ken's fingers dropped to his lap. "What's that?"

David Bachman, who stood behind his father, pumped his fist in Ken's direction. "Don't be a stick in the mud, Ken. You know who he's talking about."

I really hope not.

"Yes, yes, what's her name... Lana Losers?" If it wasn't bad enough to bring her up, Charlie said her name completely wrong. Who the fuck was Lah-na *Losers?* "That one. Everyone and their scrotums are talking about this bewitching she-devil of real estate."

Ken twitched. "I think you mean *Lay-na Low-siers.*"

"Ah, yes, her. Have you met her at all?"

Oh, if only he could count the ways in which he had met his dear Lana. Ken had done quite well not letting anyone know that he was currently the man sheathing his cock into Lana's tight abode on a daily basis. *Now I have to cross my legs extra hard thinking about it.* What a time to get a hard-on. But who could blame him? Lana was the kind of woman who sashayed into a man's imagination without warning. *She knows it, too.* That made her an even more formidable woman.

"Yes, I've met her a few times. She's hard to miss." Nobody was a bombshell like Lana, even without the perfect hair, makeup, and outfits that made her stand out in any male-dominated crowd. "Why are you so interested in her?"

He soon wished he hadn't asked that. "I hear she's quite the beauty. David here says every man is falling over himself trying to get into bed with her, if you know what I mean."

Ken was in a precarious situation. He couldn't let Charlie see any of the jealousy currently swimming within, simmering, stewing, waiting for the perfect moment to burst from Ken's throat and make it known that Lana Losers was *his*. *Yeah, mine to lose.* Things were going so well between them. Why did she have to leave in the morning? Would Ken get to at least make love to her one last time?

Nope. He couldn't let Charlie in on any of this. As much as Ken wanted to swing his dick around like a caveman with his

A Fated Night

first ever hard-on, he had to remain professional for his sake and secretive for Lana's. The last thing she needed was for her conference lover to kiss and tell.

Even if he really, really wanted to punch his boss in the face for even implying such a foul thing about Lana's personal life.

"She is quite… fetching." Ken would have to hope he both acknowledged Lana's beauty and managed to not let his real attraction to her show. "And very intelligent. The few times I've spoken to her have been eye-opening. She didn't get her title by accident."

"No, I had my man Garrett take a look at her figures the moment I realized she was going to be a hot commodity on the employment market. The woman made two million more than the guy who got second place. *And* the young man who got second was selling much more valuable properties than she was. A woman doesn't get there on accident."

"I'm sure she'll wander through this room soon enough."

"Yeah, Dad, you'll know it's her and not another hotel guest because half the guys in the room will be following her like dogs."

Ken glared at David. "Is there a point to all of this? Or did you come to participate in the hen-house gossip too, Charlie?"

"Come on, Ken, lighten the hell up." Charlie leaned forward. "What I want is Lana Losers on my roster. Get a meeting with her tonight and make her an offer."

David's grin implied that he already knew about this scheme. Ken, on the other hand, flipped his binder shut and tossed it into the tote bag at his feet.

"What kind of *offer* am I to make, Charlie?"

"Ken, I don't care if you have to eat her cunt to get her to take a one million dollar sign-on bonus and a starting salary of one-fifty a year. Get on your knees like a man and please that Mary Magdalene so she'll move to New York for us and make us richer."

The breath in Ken's chest staled. Every time he tried to breathe, he was faced with some kind of clog in his throat. "I don't think that's a good idea."

"Why the hell not? Don't you want the commissions that trickle up to you when your agents succeed?"

"Of course I do. I'm simply not convinced that Lana will mesh well with the team we currently have."

"What are you talking about? They'll love her! They'll be taking her out for drinks the first Friday she works!"

"Yes, that's what I'm afraid of. She'll be a distraction, Charlie."

"I can't believe you're saying this, Mr. Feminist." Well, it had been a while since Ken was chided with that title. All because he stood up against the sexual harassment the secretaries and assistants at Lois & Bachman were dealing with from a former agent. "Come on, Kenneth! It's the new millennium. Women can be hard-hitting real estate agents too. Hehe." Charlie looked over his shoulder and to his youngest son. "Did that sound convincing, David?"

"Absolutely, Dad."

"See?" Charlie chuckled. "Even David's on board." His voice dropped into a more serious tone. "I want to make sure there's no mistaking my intent here, Andrews." How many iterations of Ken's name were they going to go through? "I. Want. Her. If I find out you didn't meet her tonight to offer her a job, I swear to God, I'll put your head on a spike."

Charlie wasn't playing around, either. He often kidded with people he liked – which included Ken – but he could be ruthless when necessary. The only reason he cut that agent was to avoid the legal charges heading his way. If Charlie Bachman said he wanted Lana Losers on his payroll? Ken would do everything in his power short of holding a gun to Lana's head to make it happen. The figures Bachman were offering were not chump change, either. No doubt their biggest competitors would try to throw their own figures at her, but Ken doubted they would come close to a million on sign and a hundred and fifty grand a year to start with. That was almost as much as Ken made before commissions.

"Ah," Charlie stood up with the help of his son, "I can't wait to say I have that hot piece of ass making me richer. Watch out, son, you might have a new stepmother soon."

Ken managed to maintain his composure until his boss and accompanying son were far enough away to not pay him any mind. Once he was alone, he threw his bags together and hunted down an old colleague of his. Anything to take his mind off Lana.

***

That late afternoon marked the final formal event of the conference. Everyone who cared to attend filed into the biggest room to watch Lana Losers accept her award as the best-selling real estate agent in the designated region of New England.

Since everyone with a working libido had a crush on her, the room was packed.

Ken heard the whispers as he sat toward the back by himself. "That Lana sure is a hottie," two men in front of him muttered. "I hear Lois & Bachman are going to make an offer." They glanced back at Ken and then kept their mouths shut.

"Is it true that Esperanza Realty has already offered her a job? Roger Prescott is going to be rich from the headhunter's fee on that one."

"There's going to be a bidding war between Holts & Graham and Boya Realty Group."

"I'll eat my hat if she isn't competing against us here in Manhattan in less than a year. Because what we really need right now is a ringer against us and Lois & Bachman. Those assholes are enough of a problem."

"How do you think she sells so much? Does she actually offer sexual favors to get an edge over her competition?"

"How have you never heard of this woman yet? She's going to be bigger than Madonna at Madison Square Garden."

"I know an easy way to take someone like her out of commission. Put a baby in her."

The uproarious laughter gave Ken a headache. He was glad when the room was quieted so the chairman of the conference could give his speech and introduce Lana to receive her reward.

A Fated Night

She had changed since Ken last saw her. A navy blue dress wrapped around her curvaceous figure, showing enough cleavage to entice her enemy without being too garish. Black slingback shoes graced her petite feet as she stepped onto the stage. Lana flashed the whole room a grin as big as her personality before stopping to pause for a picture. She shook the chairman's hand and received a framed document citing her accomplishments for the years 2002-2003. More photo ops. Every flash of the camera and the ripples of applause that commenced only made her face light up more in genuine pride.

She should be proud. Ken remained leaning back in his chair, far back and short enough that Lana probably couldn't see him. Although he swore her eyes searched the room more than once. *Not everyone breaks the kind of records that she has.* Not everyone got the kind of job offers that Ken was supposed to give her.

No, no. He couldn't do that. Her working for him would never, well, work.

Lana stood at the podium, absentmindedly pushing hair out of her face and occasionally giggling in excitement. When she dropped the cold, professional façade, she let the world see a much softer side of her. That didn't work for her in the real working world. It did, however, make Ken hate himself even more.

She gave a short speech thanking the committee that awarded her for her achievements, then jumped into talking about her work history and what her plans for the future were. Ken knew he should be listening with rapt attention, considering his own history with this woman and all, but he was... distracted. With her.

Lana had become more than a gorgeous woman Ken had a conference fling with. That kind of woman wouldn't be stuck in his head for hours at a time. She wouldn't haunt him while he dined with colleagues and made plans for real estate world domination. She wouldn't blow up his email with flirtatious requests that he spank her again their last night together. *Don't give me ideas.* After what Lana did to him once the ropes switched hands? He might need a spanking too.

That was the rub, wasn't it? He had exposed much of his own sexual history and proclivities to her. The kind of stuff that sent most women he dated screaming. Finding one who made his heart flutter *and* was interested in hearing about the kinkier stuff he got involved with when he thought nobody was paying attention? Ken never thought the day would come, let alone at an innocuous conference he attended because it was conveniently located.

At first, it had been fun knowing that he was the only man at that conference who had actually managed to touch her, to kiss her, to make her come over and over again. Ken would never forget the way she sighed in his mouth when she was about to climax, or how the depths of her body loved to suck him in deeper. No, they wouldn't know because men like them didn't hold her interest. She wanted a mature man who knew when it was time to put down his work and love on her – and let her love on him. Lana liked money. She adored success. She was willing to work her ass off to gain more of both in her life.

A Fated Night

Would it be so crazy to think that she could run her own firm within another ten years? Possibly own half of Manhattan? Or were those Ken's dreams?

We could never work for the same agency. Not as equals, and not as boss and subordinate. Their work culture fostered competition. Employees who started hooking up either dropped it immediately or decided who was going to quit. Ken sleeping with Lana while they both worked for Lois & Bachman would make the other employees resentful (because clearly that meant he would show her favoritism in exchange for her pussy) and tarnish her reputation she had carefully crafted over the years. Nobody would take her accomplishments and merits seriously anymore. They would think Ken had ensured her success for his own romantic gains.

The idea was doomed. There was no way she could work for Lois & Bachman.

No, wait. There was no way they *both* could work for Lois & Bachman.

Ken's mind danced between thoughts of Lana in his bed and fantasies of the kind of life he wished to have one day. What did he really want? His own business, working for himself? A wife? A house in the countryside or a penthouse in the middle of the city? A damn dog? Six cats that constantly fought with one another? Three cars, only one of which he ever used? Live-in staff? A driver? Private jet? What the fuck did Ken *want*?

Her. He sucked in his breath when Lana stepped away from the podium for one last photo-op, her dress hugging her body like he wanted to hug her in turn. *I want her. Forever.*

The bastard was in love. In as little as three days the fates had conspired to pair him with the only woman who could ever be his real equal, both professionally and sexually. If he couldn't find a way to make something work between them, he might as well give up everything he had worked for. Because what would be the point, otherwise?

***

Lana soaked up the adoration of those around her with both appreciation and indifference. Of course she wanted to have her accomplishments acknowledged. What extroverted woman *wouldn't?* She feasted on the energy of the men and few women around her. *I'll eat them all alive on the market.* Yet she kept her smile pleasant and her words kind as she shook some hands and thanked everyone who told her she was an inspiration. Particularly one young female real estate agent who came up to her and declared her a role model for all women like them everywhere.

Well, that wouldn't go to Lana's head at all!

She was so caught up in her jubilation that she sometimes forgot to look for Ken. Where was her sweetheart? Was that him sitting in the back by himself? Why did he look so damn glum? Didn't he know that she was getting horny enough from all this attention that he could take her into the nearest closet and bang her brains out? Like he did last night? Like he did in the shower this morning?

Lana turned away from him and talked with two reporters. Roger Prescott shadowed her, declaring her the most valuable asset to ever hit his company. To that end, he publicly announced that Lana would soon be a free agent for the benefit of her career. Oh, and he was looking for her replacement in his DC agency. Did anyone happen to know some young, dashing agent looking for a good gig?

A line of representatives from varying firms came up to shake her hand again. The Californians once again implied she could be on TV. Someone else asked if she ever thought about going to Europe. *I don't know anything substantial about the real estate there. Let me stick to the stomping grounds I know I can conquer.* Even in her slingbacks.

She was pleasantly surprised when Ken approached her toward the end of her stay in the room. Lana and Roger were invited to attend a cocktail party in their honor, and Roger was already going on about the margaritas he wanted to drink. With the conference over, he was game to find a young man to shack up with for the night. Assuming there were no good business dinners for him to shadow Lana on…

"Congratulations on your well-deserved reward," Ken said with a professional handshake. He kept a respectful distance from Lana. *I know we don't want people to know we're screwing, but this feels so… cold.* It definitely was not what Lana expected when she saw Ken. Or perhaps she was falling in too deep with this handsome man who had managed to abscond with her loins and possibly her heart the second time they met. "It seems that you have inspired many of the people here to actually start competing at this game."

She laughed. Roger glanced at her with disbelief. What? Like she couldn't laugh at something Ken said? *Oh, right. I rarely find men funny.* Roger knew her well enough to know what was her real laugh and what was her practiced good, amicable girl laugh. "Thank you, Mr. Andrews," Lana said. "That means a lot coming from a man of your own legacy."

"Oh? I wasn't aware that I had such a legacy."

"You're the lead manager of the #1 firm in New York. I'd say you have done quite well for yourself."

"Keep up your hard work and you'll be in my place soon enough." Ken paused. Roger steeled himself for anything other than what Ken said next. "If I may, Mr. Prescott, I'd like to briefly chat with Ms. Losers alone. I promise to have her back within five minutes."

Roger looked between them before taking several steps back. He gave Lana thumbs up, as if anything was going to happen between her and Ken in front of God and country.

Damn. She wished it would. She hadn't been lying when she told him that she was fantasizing about fucking him in public. Oh, good. Now she was thinking about it again. What a time for a woman's exhibitionist streak to come out.

"What can I do for you, Mr. Andrews?" she flashed him one of her more demure smiles. She had to be careful, though. Didn't need anyone happening to look over and recognizing that look. If she could make it out of this conference without

A Fated Night

anyone but Ken knowing what went on between them, good. That's exactly what she required at this point in her life. Still, didn't mean she didn't want his attentions…

He tucked his bag beneath his arm and offered her the wanest of smiles. "I was hoping to see you for dinner after you've put in your appearance at your party. We have much to discuss."

"Oh, do we?" Lana wasn't sure what he meant, other than making yet another bid for them to become more than a fling. *He wants to be my boyfriend. It's charming.* Lana wasn't sure she would say no, either, had they lived in the same city. At any rate, her career was getting started. Was now really the time to get serious with a guy? "I'm sure I can squeeze you in after eight. Don't forget I have a flight at one tomorrow."

"I haven't forgotten. How could I forget you leaving my fair city?"

Lana shrugged. "I really do not know, Mr. Andrews. Tell you what. I'll give you my number. For more than business."

Ken's fake demeanor dropped in surprise. Lana had him by the balls. Right where she wanted him.

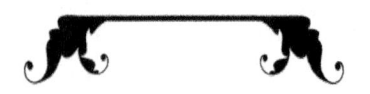

Chapter 11

"I Love You."

They kissed beneath a string of bulbous Christmas lights, the both of them aware that around the corner were a hundred conference goers having heated discussions and engaging in witty, drunken banter. If they came from the cocktail party thrown in Lana's honor, it was the latter.

I know I feel giddier than a bubbly glass of champagne. Lana refused to let Ken go. No matter how many times he attempted to break off their kiss, she pressed forward, begging him to give her another taste for a few more seconds. Why he had chosen to take her to dinner at the hotel restaurant remained a mystery, however. Lana didn't want to waste time going to a fancy restaurant blocks away, no, but would it have killed them to go back to the restaurant Ken owned? More privacy – and the illusion of seeing each other again.

A Fated Night

At least he had reserved them a private table behind an opaque glass partition. So very '80s, but in a way that screamed *You miss this decade, don't you? Here. Have it tastefully shoved in your face. We guarantee you'll love it. Perfect for romantic dates at the end of a long conference and even longer fuckfest with a man you met three days ago!*

But Lana knew that all it would take was one nosy fucker poking around the end of the partition and finding them in the act. That made kissing Ken so much hotter. Lana had swapped her makeup palette to match her royal purple cocktail dress to look good in photos. She wanted to wow him. She wanted her lipstick prints all over his collar.

"Ahem," a waiter said. Ken tensed beneath Lana's touch. She wasn't about to let him go, however. It was a waiter! What was he going to do? Tell the whole restaurant that they were making out? Lana moved her lips from Ken's throat to his clothes, leaving behind that lip print she desperately wanted to give that white fabric. "I'm afraid we're out of the 1933. May I recommend the 1927? Another fine year."

Ken agreed to anything. Lana was happy to curl her arm around him again for more kisses. Sure, she'd have to disengage to eat a dinner she starved for, but until then, she was in full date mode.

For some reason, Ken was not in a hurry to keep their play going. As soon as the waiter left, doing his best to not blush at how randy two guests were, Ken sat back in his seat with a sigh. "I'd like to talk, if you don't mind," he said to Lana.

"So would I." Lana was going to save it until later, but she went ahead and popped open her wallet laying in her bag. She pulled out her keycard and slid it across the table. When Ken looked at her suspiciously, she said, "For later. It's my spare. I plan on getting tipsy enough on that wine you ordered that I might need help getting into my room."

Ken stared at the card for a second longer than Lana anticipated. *Is something wrong?* Lana set her worries aside when Ken finally pocketed the card. "A naughty woman as always, Lana."

She cupped her hand over his on the table. "There's something else I want to talk about."

"Hm?"

"I've been thinking." Lana fingered the rim of the votive candleholder flickering in the center of the table. "About, um, us."

Ken's fingers curled into a fist beneath Lana's hand.

"What have you been thinking?"

"Are you serious about wanting to date? I mean, beyond tomorrow?"

Those fingers uncurled again, overturning Lana's hand and squeezing her fingers. "I wouldn't suggest something like that lightly."

"I had hoped you would say that. Because you were right, you know? I'm probably moving to New York by the end of the year. Depends on who I decide to work for and when I can start, let alone make moving arrangements."

"About that..."

"No, no, let me continue. So it may be a few months before I can permanently move to New York, but would a few months really be hard to casually date? I mean, if you're willing to come down to DC when you can, I'm sure I'll be in and out of JFK for interviews." Lana had thought about this all day. Because the thought of letting go of a man like Ken and possibly never seeing him again hurt. *Come on, I'm not gonna say something like that…* What was she? Irrevocably foolish? "It doesn't even have to be 'serious' dating. If you wanna see other people on the side…"

"Lana." His fingers threaded with hers. "If there's a woman like you thinking about me somewhere in the world, then I can't imagine thinking about anyone else. We could talk about what we really want from a more serious relationship when you move here."

How could she not smile to hear that? "Come on, I know you've got the words in you."

"Come again?"

She tittered as if she couldn't believe she had to lead him on. "Are you going to ask me to be your girlfriend?"

"That's a bit traditional for you."

"Sure is. Now ask me so I can say yes."

Ken looked down, lips turning inward, outward, trapped between his teeth. "Would you be my girlfriend, Lana?"

She snuck him a kiss before the waiter returned with their new bottle of wine.

There were a million things to talk about, and none of them had to do with work. Lana wanted to know everything he had time to tell her. Now that she knew this would not be their last night together, she was able to breathe easier. Enjoy herself.

Take her time to ask Ken everything she had found curious about him. What were his brother's names? He had how many nephews already? Where was his family from? Denmark? That was random, wasn't it? What were his ten-year plans? Did he really think he could start running his own company by forty? Did he want kids? Was there pressure in his family to have kids?

And what did he think about certain forms of *love?*

Lana asked her questions with one hand on his thigh and the other propping up her chin. She was so infatuated with every answer he gave her that the dinner flew by. What did she eat? She never remembered. Was it good? Must have been okay enough to not distract her from her new boyfriend. Did she spend half her dinner rubbing his thighs in the hopes of getting him erect? Oh, yes.

She talked about her own family during the last part of dinner. Ken remained silent, occasionally nodding, asking questions, and making blithe comments. Somehow, he became more distanced as the minutes wore on and Lana's throat grew parched. Luckily, she was more than happy to drink her share of the wine. The woman wanted to be tipsy, after all. *I'm going to fuck him so hard tonight.* Thoughts like that made her giggle and tap her bare foot against his shin. *I want to ride him in a chair first. Then bend over my hotel bed and get it good. I wonder if it's too early for anal?* She didn't mean for her.

Oh, there were so many things for them to do! Lana needed to stop getting ahead of herself. She promised her fantasies that there would be plenty of time to act them out now that they were a couple willing to make the temporary distance work.

"Who are you thinking of working for?" Ken asked in a rare lull. Lana was soothing her throat with more wine. "I'm sure you've had some offers by now. Maybe I could tell you something about the firms. I know them all."

"Well." Lana hadn't wanted to talk about work, but it was relevant to their relationship, she supposed. "Nothing official, no. But Roger told me some 'good news' during the cocktail party earlier." Which Ken had skipped out on, she noted. "Wyman Group is offering me a hundred sign on, moving costs covered, their full insurance package, and even a big deal on rent if I move into a place owned by Saul Wyman."

"I see." Ken considered his glass of wine. "What about the salary?"

"Also a hundred grand a year."

"Any other offers?"

Lana went over the other two she knew of, although the details were fuzzy. When she finished speaking, Ken downed the last of his wine and said, "You know, if you worked for a place like Lois & Bachman, I bet they'd treat you the best out of them all."

"What are you talking about?" She scoffed. "I'm not working for them. We decided, remember?"

"Yes, I remember." Ken squeezed her hand. "But what if I told you that they're blowing those offers out of the water?"

Lana released his hand, sitting back in her seat with nothing but confusion to accompany her. "Excuse me?" *What is this?*

Why are we talking about me working for your company? Did you forget that's impossible if I'm your girlfriend? "I know you're not offering me a *job* right now, Ken."

"I'm not." Ken signed for the bill to be added to his company's tab. *What is he doing? He wouldn't risk his company knowing about this dinner unless… unless…*

Unless they had already signed off on it. This was officially a business dinner.

"Then what the fuck are you on about?" Did he feel her ire? Did it burn him like her being truly pissed at him would light his balls on fire? Ken hadn't seen that side of her. *Don't make me show you that side of myself, Kenneth Andrews.* He wouldn't like that side of her. "Did your boss sic you on me? I swear to God…"

He quickly leaned in toward her, hand on her arm. "Yes. Are you happy? Yes. Charlie Bachman showed up and told me to hire you so help me God. They're willing to pay you more money than you make in six months working for Prescott. To sign on. They want to treat you like a fucking queen, Lana. You'd be an *idiot* to go to any other company for the relative peanuts. You're worth more than that."

"Worth more than…" Lana gasped. How dare he! Really! How dare he! Implying she was some whore who could be bought, sold, and traded to the highest bidder in the game. Bad enough she felt like cattle already. Did she have to feel like a piece of sexual meat too?

Oh, God.

That was what hurt the most.

A Fated Night

In a single instance, the fantasy dissipated. The dates. The flirting. The *sex*. Ken Andrews wasn't her boyfriend! He wasn't even a simple convention fling!

The fucker had been buttering her up for a *job offer!*

That was the story exploding in Lana's head, and she refused to believe anything else. From the moment she leaped up from her seat and looked the liar in the eye, she felt so… so *stupid*. How could she believe he wanted her for anything other than mere sex? To be his girlfriend! Yeah, so she would work for Lois & Bachman, no matter how bad of an idea that was!

"Lana, please…" Ken held up his hands in a futile effort to calm her down.

"Fuck off, you piece of shit." Why was the wine gone? She would love to splash some on his face! Instead, Lana would have to make do with her dirty napkin, which she threw with gusto. "I can't believe I fell for you. All of that… what we *did*… God!" She grabbed her purse and marched out from behind the partition, facing a hotel restaurant gallery full of half-drunk convention goers… including Roger Prescott cozying up to Charlie and David Bachman.

The. Bastards.

"Lana!" Roger called. She hurried past him, shooting both father and son of the Bachman fuckers the biggest stink eye to stain her face. "Where are you going? Come say hello to Charlie Bachman! You know, of Lois & Bachman?"

His voice was lost in the laughter and clinking glasses of the restaurant and neighboring bar. Terrible, embarrassing memories took Lana over. *This bar is where we met. This is where I decided to fuck him.* How could she be so foolish?

Apparently, she could easily be foolish.

Lana raced up to her room, keycard fumbling in the lock until she screamed in frustration. She bottled up another scream until she could collapse on her bed and shove her face in her feathery pillow.

She didn't expect to follow that scream with gross, ugly tears that felt like they were drowning the heart she had so carefully shielded until now.

***

Lana attempted to force sleep. She told herself that she would get up early, check out of the hotel before most of the other attendees roused themselves, and bide her time at the airport lounge until it was time to fly back to DC. *That's it. Think of your apartment in DC.* Ken did not exist in DC. He was a misfortune of the year, but at least he hadn't tainted Lana's personal stomping grounds. To think she had invited him down to spend time with her…

To think she had agreed to be his girlfriend.

Lana could handle being used. Used for sex? Even less offensive. Not like she didn't run around using men for sex all the time. But those situations had a mutual understanding that declared sex to be the only thing on the table. Never Lana's heart, which she kept as guarded as a diamond in a lockbox.

A Fated Night

She had transgressed her own boundaries. Ken was not meant to be anything more than sex and some trite conversations. Maybe he would offer her his honest opinion on the places she could work. Once they had established they could not work together due to their chemistry, however, Lana had grown too complacent.

Her heart was ripped open for a man to grab for his own. *No, no, what have I done?* Lana couldn't sleep. She rolled back and forth in her hotel bed, wishing that this had not been where she and Ken first made love. *What am I doing, thinking about it like that? What am I? Nuts?* Nuts in love?

No, no, no…

Lana intermittently cried from the moment she went to bed until she finally got up to use the bathroom. She stood in front of the mirror, cleaning up her makeup and hygiene products so she wouldn't have to do it in the morning. A bedraggled, red-eyed face looked back at her. White cotton negligee. Pink silk robe that was barely longer than her nightgown. Haggard blond hair already tangled. Drooping posture. Tear tracks on her cheeks. *Get it out now.* Get out all the tears she would bother shedding over Kenneth Andrews and his backstabbing ways.

Telling her there was nothing professional between them…

Making her feel like that during sex…

Asking her to be his girlfriend and promising to make the long distance work until she was securely in New York for her new job, regardless of who she worked for…

Then offering her a job to work at his company! Beneath *him!*

Did he think she wouldn't notice? That she would go on in ignorant bliss thinking that he wasn't pitching Lois & Bachman over all the other nice offers she received? Was that his plan all along? Seduce her, fuck her, use his dick to get her to work for him and make him richer? The man already owned half the neighborhood. He didn't need her to make him money!

He got the girl and the prestige of hiring her. He got to do two things nobody else at the conference could achieve. His ego must've been the size of Manhattan right now, regardless if Lana stormed out on him or not.

She rolled toward the window and stared at the view she hadn't bothered to cover up with the curtains before going to bed. *Do I want to move to a city where a man like that rules?* Personally? No. Professionally? Hell yes she did. Lana wanted to move to New York and become Ken Andrews's biggest enemy. She wanted to become so powerful in their industry that she could start buying *his* properties. She would start with the hotel next door. Raze it to the ground. Goodbye, fucker.

Lana was stewing in these ridiculous fantasies when she heard her room door open.

She froze in her bed. *Am I hearing things?* It took her a few seconds to remember she had given Ken a copy of her keycard.

He...

He wasn't...

"Lana." A dark figure stood at the end of her bed. "I know you're awake."

Why oh why did she react? She shouldn't have kicked her foot out from beneath the covers!

A Fated Night

"Stalker," she muttered. "You could've left the card at the front desk."

He leaned against the bed. "I'm sorry. You need to listen to me. I…"

"Shut up. Turn around. Leave. Never speak to me again." Lana grabbed her cell phone off the nightstand. "Don't make me call security. I will, you *asshole.*"

"Let me explain myself first. Then I'll leave."

Lana curled her legs closer to the rest of her body. *Don't touch me. If you try to touch me, I swear to God…*

"My boss made me bring it up. I didn't want to. I… I'm so sorry, Lana."

She choked on the tears reemerging from her eyes. "You bastard."

"I deserve that. I shouldn't have brought it up. I should've been honest about my boss and told you to lie about being asked to cover both of our asses. I broke your trust in me."

Did he think that was enough to apologize? Because he *hadn't* been straightforward with her. He had spent their whole romantic dinner thinking about how he was going to weasel the question in her direction so he could technically tell his boss he had asked her to join Lois & Bachman. That wasn't honesty. That was the work of a man who only cared about his own image. Lana was all too familiar with those kinds of guys.

"You've apologized. I'm not obligated to accept it, though. You can leave now."

"Lana…"

She sat up, tangled hair a mess all over her shoulders and on her forehead. She was glad the lights were off and he couldn't see the terrible state she was in. *I hate you. We should be in bed together right now, talking about who is going to visit who first. Then I'd fuck you again.* It wasn't fair. The one time she decided to trust a jerk, and it immediately bit her in the ass.

Lana couldn't believe she was fast-tracking herself to falling in love with this motherfucker.

It was so dark in her room, save for the lights twinkling through the window, that she could barely see him. He didn't wear a jacket. Just his gray vest and his shirt half untucked from his trousers. While she couldn't see his face, Lana instinctively knew that there wasn't a bit of happiness on his countenance. Good. He should feel shitty about what he had done to her. Lana wasn't in the business of easy forgiveness. She wouldn't have made it as far as she had otherwise.

Still, what the fuck was that pull to him? Was he really so pathetic that she couldn't help but stare at his darkened form, waiting for him to leave? Hoping he would do something, anything to make her happy again? *Don't do this. Please.* Lana didn't need to act this way over a man. She would cry for a night, harden her heart again, and then move the fuck on. Maybe she would go straight to the club when she got home and use her Monday night to shack up with some piece of ass she would never know the name of. Man, woman, she didn't care. As long as they didn't look or smell like Ken…

Or taste like him..

Or *feel* like him…

A Fated Night

Panic overcame Lana. Not for her safety, but for the unbelievable idea that maybe, just maybe, she wasn't ready to let him go yet.

It's over. It never really began. Your conference fling, asshole. There he is. Looking smug... maybe not so smug... I don't know.

Lana hung her head, willing her tangles to obscure the man she couldn't bear to look at. Why hadn't he left yet? Why was he torturing her with his presence? All she wanted was to be left alone to stew in her own misery. Misery that *he* caused!

"You know it's over, right?" Who invited the frog chorus into her throat? Pathetic.

He shifted between his feet. "Yeah. I know. I didn't really entertain the idea that you would forgive me. I fucked up."

Why did he have to say the right thing? *Hold to your convictions, girl.* Lana placed one hand in front of her, clutching the bedding. "I hate you right now," she admitted. "I hate what you've done to me."

Ken made a tight fist with his right hand. How similar was it to that fist he grabbed her with at the dinner table? "I'll say that I'm sorry again, then. It wasn't right to make you feel led on."

"I'm not talking about that." Lana sniffed. "Fuck you. You know what I mean. This whole week... you've fucked with me. Not just my cunt. You fucked with my head!" She lifted her eyes, unfurling a flurry of daggers from the depths of her mind. "You fucked with my heart!"

She wished she could see his expression. She was also grateful that she didn't have to.

"You made all those promises! You said we could try for a relationship no matter what. You made me actually believe something like that was possible! How could you? How could you fuck with me like that? I don't care how sorry you are. You don't go back on me like that. All you did was show me that I really don't know who the fuck you are." Really, how stupid had she been? Thinking that she could have a relationship with a man she carnally knew more than she knew about his history, his likes and dislikes, what he did when he wasn't working and bedding women, anything like that… she knew *nothing*. Lana Losers did not walk into professional or personal relationships without seeing them from all angles first. She didn't let her heart rule her mind like that. How could she keep her edge, otherwise?

"I did. For what it's worth, I really did believe them."

"Fuck off. I don't know what to believe about *you* anymore."

"That's fair. I'll… I'll go now. Good luck with whatever you decide to do."

He turned, taking three long steps toward the front of her hotel room. Lana braced herself against the bed, wanting to fall face first… wanting to suffocate herself in the upturned sheets. Even now, her heart furiously beat, begging her to somehow *fix this* before she regretted her unfortunate decisions for the rest of her life.

What if she could have it? What if she could have both the sexual connection and an emotional layer that made it even better? What if something like romantic love was true? Lana

A Fated Night

was in her late 20s, but she had never been *in love* before. She didn't think it was possible anymore. If she hadn't experienced that emotion that made her choke on her every drop of spit in her throat and ache between her legs every time the man was in the room... then what hope was there that she ever would?

That man who did this to her was walking away now. While her mind counseled her that this was the best thing to let transpire, her heart screamed at her to *fix this right now, you fucking stupid harpy.*

"Wait!"

What had she done?

Ken looked over his shoulder at her. She hadn't seen it before, but she saw it now: desperation. Cold, hot, desperation.

They didn't say another word. Neither of them. No words except mumbled, whispered, and hushed *Yeses, Nos,* and *Pleases.* Even then, those words melted around Lana's brain, seizing, holding it hostage in an attempt to get it to shut up. Her heart was in control now. Her stupid, foolish heart that begged her to not let Ken walk away before he made love to her one last time.

Raw and dirty. That's how Lana often liked her sex, but she had never embraced the type of raw and dirty she did tonight. Perhaps it was her heart that was the rawest, her skin the dirtiest when covered in dried tears and the grease of her unwashed hair. Ken's cologne was muted. Tobacco colored his clothes and breath. Yet that was also the scent of the late spring New York City night. How long had he walked around outside, trying to clear his head of her? *He couldn't do it. He came here in the end. He can't be without me, can he?*

She wanted every piece of him. *I know I can't have them now.* She wanted to feel his whole body fuck her the hell up. *It's the last time it will ever mean something.* She wanted to taste that desperation perspiring from within. *It's so bitter, yet hopeful.* She wanted to feel him in one of the most self-destructive ways possible. If this was her last time making love to Ken Andrews, she wanted it as natural as possible. She was going to commit every second to memory, burning it there until she died – and it was the last memory to flash before her eyes.

"You sure?" He slammed his hand down on her thigh the moment the condom was knocked from his hand.

Lana answered with a greedy kiss to his wet and hungry lips. "Make me come so hard I never forget you," she said.

He felt so good inside of her.

They were a riot of shaking limbs and wrinkled clothes that had refused to fully come off. The bedcovers were knocked to the floor. The back of Lana's head was married to the space between her pillows, Ken's body surging against her so primally that she had no choice but to surge back up against him. It was probably some sort of sign that her body easily welcomed him in, because regardless of how tight she was when he first entered, she was nothing but a slut for him now.

That's how she chose to see this final encounter with Ken. *I'm a slut, and sluts fuck men they shouldn't, right?* She shouldn't be doing this, but she couldn't help herself. His touch, although hard and sometimes rough as he held her down and fucked her with his bare cock, was almost worshipful. Maybe Ken couldn't be the one any longer, but he wouldn't leave her without making Lana feel that he *somewhat* made up for his indiscretions. "*See?*" he seemed to say with nothing more than the way he commanded his body, "*I make you feel this good. You're a fucking goddess in my eyes. Take what little offerings I have and turn them into something amazing.*" His suffocating kisses almost destroyed her.

If all that mattered was how good it felt physically, then she could survive what her heart did to her later. Ah, but it wasn't so easy, was it? Every time he thrust into her, she experienced a type of euphoria that killed every negative thought swarming her mind. When he pulled out, even slightly, she feared he would leave her forever, that this was the last time they would ever touch. *Don't go. I need you. I need to feel like this for the rest of my life.* What the fuck was her heart doing butting into her business again? Didn't it have any shame? Maybe Lana wanted to end her conference hookup with the best bang possible!

No woman wanted to cry during sex. Least of all Lana, who had been conditioned to see crying – especially in front of men, let *alone* in her industry – as the ultimate physical sign of weakness. And, no, she did not cry. Technically. No sobbing. No sounds except moans and cries of ecstasy. But there were two, maybe three tears working their way down her cheek again, and she had no excuse other than attributing them to the fear she had that she would feel so alone for the rest of her life.

Ken was relentless. From the second he was first inside of her, he never stopped, never let up, never let Lana experience any side of him except for the one that had to have her. He didn't give her much chance to speak. His lips were always on hers, muffling those cries she emitted and tasting the depths of her throat.

"I'm coming," she whimpered. Her toes were curling and her core pined for relief. Every muscle between her breasts and thighs alit in a fire that only Ken could put out. All she needed was one thing to send her over the edge. His thickening cock shoved to the hilt within her wasn't enough.

He put his mouth on her nipple, biting. Lana groaned from the insanity it brought her. The core of her body grabbed onto his cock in a mad attempt to pull him in deeper, one more time.

"Me too," Ken admitted with a hushed tone. "I can't... I can't let you go."

Good. Lana didn't want him to. She wanted to play Russian Roulette with nature. Fate had already conspired to bring them together. It would always find some other way.

"Lana!"

The harried cry of a man on the brink of losing everything he ever thought of himself sounded into her skull. Lana waited, most impatiently, for the brunt of his climax to wreck her irrevocably. *Make me feel something I'll never get to know again.*

"Ken..."

She was on another planet. With him.

God. So deep. That cock was giving her as much as it could. His seed hit her in a place so intimate that she shuddered beneath Ken's weight. Darkness washed over her eyes. Most women spoke of seeing white lights. Not Lana. She knew she was in trouble because all she saw was shadow, like a winter night sky.

A Fated Night

Ken had managed to completely blackout her thoughts. For the rest of the night, she wouldn't have to think about anything.

He continued to slowly fuck her long past the end of his orgasm. Lana remained prostrate, arms either wrapped around his head or futilely searching for his shoulders. She both wanted him to make himself scarce and to never, ever abandon her.

"I love you."

She had misheard him, right? Lana opened her eyes, seeing nothing but a mess of his black hair as he sucked the exposed part of her throat. Damn. This should've been the pinnacle of romantic. Heaven knew Lana needed to know what this felt like.

Then he was out of her, off of her. Ken left a lingering kiss on her lips before getting up and putting his clothes back together.

"What did you say?"

He sat on the edge of the bed, head dropping. "Lois & Bachman are offering you a million to sign on and a hundred and fifty salary before commissions. You'd be making almost as much money as me. You'd be a damned fool to not work for them. They'll treat you right, especially if they want you so badly."

"But…"

"The day you start working there will be the day I resign. Don't worry about me. This has all shown me that I need to get serious about my own career. Like you're being held back at

Prescott's firm, I'm being held back by Lois & Bachman." He stood. "I'll see you around, Lana. Maybe we'll… goodbye."

Whatever he was going to say was consumed by the air. Ken showed himself out of Lana's room with the flurry of a man with something to hide.

She remained in her exact position for who knew how long. At some point, Lana reached between her legs and felt the last remaining part of her that was warm. The rest of her skin had chilled. But the essence of her union to a man named Kenneth Andrews remained as hot as the passion always burning between them.

Even so, it was the closest thing to closure she was going to get. She would have to accept it, and maybe move on.

Chapter 12

"Do You Want Me?"

Ken didn't know how long he had, but he figured now was as good a time as any to draft his resignation letter to Lois & Bachman.

He had already called his accountant (at midnight, no less) to set up a meeting for the next day. Unfortunately, his accountant was in Miami for unrelated business, but promised to squeeze Ken in if he was willing to fly down. So Ken booked the first flight he could find out of JFK the next day and went to work laying down plans for his future.

It was better than thinking about Lana. Better to stay up all night obsessing over facts and figures than to toss and turn in bed with thoughts of the woman who had made off with his heart like the temptress she always claimed to be. So not fair. What was Ken supposed to do with his life now? *I fucked up. I fucked up so badly.* There she was, the most beautiful, vibrant woman in the world, and he had destroyed the tenuous trust between them. He knew that Lana did not love easily. That was something any man with half a brain could tell from one look in her direction. For her to open herself up to the hardships of a long distance relationship like that? To make him ask her to be his girlfriend so she could play coy before answering in the affirmative? How was she really feeling about him to be able to say that?

Ken had to let her go. It was best this way, wasn't it? Let Lana go to work at Lois & Bachman. She would thrive there, thanks to the deep pockets that made sure only the best in the business worked there. Even if she decided she couldn't bear to work there thanks to Ken's legacy, she would still have the experience and references to set her career up for life. *Why didn't I propose this to her from the beginning? Why did I* fuck *it up like that?*

It had all been fate. Now fate swung in the other direction. It wasn't meant to be. Perhaps it was meant to be the impetus they needed to make drastic personal changes, but not *together*. Then again, Lana was one of the only women he had been so passionate with. That had so much chemistry with him. *I really fucked it up.* Hilariously enough, Ken was not really into ideas of fate. But as of late he was starting to come around to the idea that the universe was looking out for him, one way or another. Great.

He eventually crashed around two in the morning, long past his usual bedtime. At first Ken didn't know *how* he was

A Fated Night

going to get any sleep. But, he supposed, the day had been long, emotional, and well... he had been drained of half his energy when he saw Lana only a few hours ago.

Can't believe I did that. He had those thoughts as he drifted off to sleep. *I never have unprotected sex. What the fuck?* Lana had that kind of hold on him, he supposed. Either that or his cock was suddenly into risky business that could give him little Kennthlings, or worse, the sort of thing that put him in the grave. Lana had mentioned being on birth control, but was it enough?

"You think I'm not responsible?"

Ken knew he was dreaming. Not only was Lana there, dressed in a pure white evening gown and threading her manicured nails through her soft blond hair, but they weren't anywhere near New York. Ken wasn't sure if it was a real location at all – or some fantasy he cooked up when in deep sleep. Even so, he was relieved to see the beloved he let get away giving him some much needed reassurance.

"I didn't mean to imply that." Ken sat at the other end of the couch. Also white. Was this supposed to be heaven? "I know you're a responsible woman." He slid his hand into the split of her dress. Was she this warm and soft in real life? Or was that the comfort of his bed making him think everything felt as good?

"Ah, Kenny." Damn, she had to be the first woman to call him that and *not* irk him. "You know why you pissed me off, right?" She touched the tip of his nose.

"You're a volatile woman who is easy to distrust others."

"I'm fun, aren't I?"

"I don't mind it."

"Even though you told me that I could take the job and you would simply walk away from yours," Lana continued. The dream iteration of her was apparently not listening. "Neither of us would really be happy with that arrangement. What, you think I want to spend the rest of my life working for others? I'm bigger than that. I'm worth more than that."

"Of course you are. I fully expect to be competing with you within ten years. My only advice is that you reconsider naming your firm. Maybe partner up with someone named Wieners."

Lana flicked the top of his hand. "Why not make me your partner?"

Ken awoke with a start. Sunshine streamed through his window, blinding him from the number on his clock.

His plane was supposed to take off in two hours.

***

"We will be ready to take off within a few more minutes, ladies and gentlemen." Every time the flight attendant spoke, Lana got another headache. This was the third time they had been delayed. At this rate she would *not* be back in DC before dinner. Not with traffic sure to fuck up her cab ride home. *I should stay at the airport until rush hour is over.* It was going to be a long day, and she was due back at work tomorrow. "We're currently waiting for one last passenger who has been held up by unforeseen circumstances."

A Fated Night

What a bitch! Lana was willing to bet that it was some woman who was held up in the toilet because her period shits got the best of her. *Always assume the grossest, and you're usually right.* At least there was one thing on Lana's side: the First Class seat next to hers was empty. The flight may have only been an hour long, but she would take what she could get.

A man in a suit and carrying an overnight bag hurried through the door. Immediately a flight attendant closed it, and Lana kept her eyes down, wondering if she should read a book or take a nap.

The late passenger stood next to her seat. *Are you kidding me?* She dropped her bag and looked up.

No.

No way.

Ken dumped his overnight bag into his First Class seat the moment he saw Lana. If she entertained any thoughts that he was stalking her, that he had conspired to make this happen on purpose, those thoughts were purged when she saw the exploding surprise on his face.

"Sir?" A flight attendant appeared. "Can I help you with that, sir? We really need to take off."

"What are you doing here?" Lana couldn't look away from him, even with the flight attendant now fussing with Ken's overnight bag. Once his seat was cleared, he sat down, showing her his ticket.

"*New York JFK to Miami MIA, temporary stop in Washington IAD.*" Lana had heard announcements detailing that her plane was going on to Miami after she was let off in DC, but that still didn't explain why… who…

"Have a last minute business meeting in Miami." Ken pocketed his ticket and buckled up his seatbelt. His skin was flushed a beet red even though he tried to play everything as cool as possible. "I honestly had no idea that you were on this flight. Let alone that we would be sitting next to each other."

"I should hope not." Lana held herself to the wall and crossed her legs away from him. "This has got to be some sick joke."

She tore open her bag only to have a flight attendant chastise her to put it away until they were in the air. Lana threw it back beneath the seat in front of her with a huff. *I must be dreaming. I fell asleep in my seat and am dreaming about Ken come to fuck with my head.*

"You know." He stared straight ahead. "It almost feels like fate."

Lana chomped on her lip, tasting the wax of her makeup. After waking up feeling more bedraggled than a wet cat, she took care to wash her hair and do her makeup just so. She was determined to waltz back into DC with nothing but perfection leading the way. "There's no such thing as fate," she grumbled.

"I used to think that." He finally glanced at her. "Yet here we are."

Something bothered her. No, Ken's presence wasn't the primary thing making her want to bite her nails and have a fit. *The Lana that was falling in love with him is dead now. This is the real Lana, checking in. She wants to deck him. Choke him. Make him choke*

A Fated Night

on her metaphorical dick because that's what he is. What bothered her was something she kept thinking about from the night before.

"So you love me, huh?"

She had pulled out a magazine and was absentmindedly flipping through it. She licked her fingers and bobbed her foot as the plane taxied down the runway. Pretty soon she would have a queasy stomach and a sinus headache. Bet Ken wouldn't be too impressed with that side of her.

"I said that, huh?"

Lana glanced at the other passengers. Luckily, nobody was paying attention to them, and the plane was too loud for people to eavesdrop anyway. "You sure did. If I didn't know any better, I'd think you *were* stalking me. I mean, you own half of Fifth Avenue, apparently. I'm surprised you don't have your own private plane. You must have called your buddies in the TSA to tell you how to find me. Did they hold this seat for you too?"

"I have no friends in the TSA. I bought this ticket last night. It was the only one available today." He grimaced. "Well, that wasn't in *Coach*."

"You're so full of shit."

"Does that mean you don't believe me when I say that I love you?"

The magazine slipped from Lana's fingers. "Don't joke about things like that."

He took her hand. The plane sped up. Anxiety took control of Lana's brain, but she didn't know if it was because Ken was being affectionate, or because the plane was about to take off.

"I would never," he softly said. "I'm not ready to let you go, Lana. I'm going down to Miami to talk with my accountant about breaking off on my own."

She shuddered, like she had shuddered beneath his body the night before. "You're going to kill me, Kenny."

His grip on her faltered. "Come again?"

Why had she called him that? Lana was so uncomfortable that she had half a mind to tell the flight attendant to switch her seat with someone in Coach. *Would he follow me back there?* "So... going into business for yourself?"

He caught her discomfort like the wind catches leaves. "I'm sorry, Lana. For everything."

"Yeah, well..." She scratched her head as if that were more interesting than talking to him. "I'm over you already."

"Are you, now?"

What was with the disbelief? Men. Really. They couldn't handle a woman saying she wasn't into them anymore. "Yes. We had fun this week. But now it's time to move on."

They pushed back into their seats as the plane ascended into the air. Lana shifted her jaw so her ears would pop faster. She was so preoccupied that she almost missed Ken reaching over and plucking her necklace charm between his fingers.

"That's why you're wearing this?"

Lana swallowed, hard. Yes, she was wearing the brass rabbit pendant. *It matches my dress, okay?* Yes, that was the reason. No others. She had no other reason to give a shit about a cheap rabbit pendant given to her by the one man she considered loving.

A Fated Night

"What do you want from me?"

The plane had stabilized in the air by the time Ken answered. "I want you to tell me the truth, Lana." He released the pendant. "Do you want to be with me?"

Yes. She did.

He looked good. He smelled good. He sounded good. *He damn well felt good.* Lana felt a mental connection with him that she had never felt with a man before. She hadn't even thought it was possible to get along with a man like she got along with him. How many times had she dated a man only to want to verbally kill him because he made her life so inane? She couldn't imagine that happening with Ken.

"All I'm saying," she began, looking out the window, "is that if we try again, I'm glad it will be long distance to start with. You need to grovel a bit, Mr. Andrews."

He pulled a pen out of his inside pocket and jotted something down on a trash piece of paper he found. Once it was slipped into her hand, Lana unfolded it and read the words, *"I don't grovel. Unless you order me to, Ms. Losers."*

She plucked his pen from his fingers and wrote something back. *"You don't know who you're playing with. I've made men get so hard they would come from walking across the room to get to me."*

Ken penned a response. *"Pretty sure that's happened once already. Still, I could use a thorough demonstration sometime."*

"Only if you promise to never pull a stunt like that again." Lana glared at him when she handed the paper back.

"This is your captain speaking," a voice said. "We've reached our cruising altitude. You're free to move about."

"I promise," Ken said. "But I don't promise to always behave. I like to think fate has brought us together for other reasons."

"Hmph." Lana watched as two passengers rose from their seats to line up for the lavatories. Once they passed, she leaned in toward Ken and whispered in his ear, "You ever join the Mile-High Club?"

Ken chuckled. "When I was fifteen."

Damn. I was nineteen. Lana needed to think of something else. "You ever have a prostate-induced orgasm at three thousand feet in the air?"

Ah, there went those eyebrows. *I'm going to spend the rest of my life trying to get a rise out of him, aren't I?* "Now that I haven't done, no." He took her hand again, this time with infinite tenderness. "Why? You ever get your G-spot rammed in an airplane?"

Lana took the paper and pen again.

"Me. You. First Class lavatory in five minutes."

"Five minutes? What do we do until then?"

Get hard and wet. Lana squeezed his hand back. "Talk, I suppose."

"Good." He leaned in closer, his breath so intoxicatingly hot on her cheek. "You know what I'm going to need?" he said. "I'm going to need a partner to help me with my plans. I can't think of anyone smarter or more beguiling than you to be my business partner."

"Oh, Kenny," Lana said with a pout. "I guess you haven't heard. I was told you don't fuck where you do business."

"I do now."

A Fated Night

Lana had a lot to think about, didn't she? When she flew in for the conference a few days ago, she knew her life was going to change for the better. What she didn't expect was falling in love and having the strangest business pitch thrown at her. Going into business with Ken Andrews? She doubted such a thing would happen right away, but it certainly gave her some thoughts she never considered before.

Oh, who was she kidding? The #1 thought on her mind right now had to do with the handsome man inviting her into his hold with those come-hither eyes. She'd do him one better and kiss those lips hiding in the midst of his carefully groomed goatee.

The ice around her heart instantly melted. This was it. Lana didn't know if it really was fate that kept bringing them together, but she did know one thing.

This was the truest love she would ever experience. She'd be a fool to cast it out of her life again.

Epilogue

"Do You Want Me?"

Another bead popped off Lana's dress and rolled beneath her sister's stiletto heels. The ever-clumsy Inid slumped right down onto the floor, her puppy-dog eyes shooting her big sister a truly pathetic look.

"Oh, for fuck's sake!" Lana looked back to the mirror. The stylist had done a fantastic job getting her hair in order for her big day, but her sister had already fucked up Lana's natural part and got duct tape tangled against the nape of her neck. What was she even doing with duct tape at City Hall? "At this rate I'm evicting you from my wedding!"

"Don't be such a Bridezilla," Juliet Losers said to her daughter. She was on her fifth glass of expensive champagne already. It was a miracle she could walk in her nude flats, let alone summon the seamstress on standby to fix Lana's dress

A Fated Night

for her. "Inid's trying to help. She wants some of your good luck for herself." Juliet sniffed in her youngest's direction. "At this rate she's never getting married, let alone to anyone respectable."

What the fuck did Lana care about her sister's dating prospects? *She* was the one getting married today!

It had been two and a half years since she met Ken Andrews, the man she knew she would one day marry but never had the guts to admit to herself. Two years of dating. Lana ended up taking the job at Lois & Bachman and joining their team by the end of 2003. As Ken promised, the day she first showed up to the office, he did his due diligence showing her around and then promptly handed Charlie Bachman his letter of resignation. His last day there, he dipped Lana at his going away party and gave her the kind of kiss that broadcasted to the whole company who they were to each other. By then, they had been together for six months and were already exchanging the L word like it was hello.

He proposed on their second anniversary. A candlelit dinner in Paris overlooking the Champs-Élysées. The diamond ring was floating in her champagne when she turned around. Ken had his chin propped up on his hand and looked at her with the goofiest expression that said he doubted she would say no.

She hadn't. After collecting her bearings, she instantly said yes.

They decided to get married as soon as logically feasible. They had already been living together in Ken's apartment for three months. Now he was ready to take his business to the next level, and he needed Lana's full-time help. As soon as she announced to Charlie Bachman that she was also leaving him to start her own enterprise, he bemoaned ever meeting the two of them. They were going to clean him out of New York.

What a fool. Ken saw a bubble waiting to burst in NYC. He and Lana agreed that the best business decision was to move to a new, more economically thriving city and grow their real estate empire there. They had already bought their first building together, the place that would become their base of operations over the coming months. As soon as they got back from their honeymoon, of course.

Perhaps most women of Lana's standing would be scandalized to get married in a place like City Hall, but it was perfect for her and Ken. She wasn't partial to a huge to-do that would attract every vulture in America and Europe. Lana wanted a small, private ceremony for their immediate family members. Inid was a good enough maid of honor, and Ken's brother Travis was serving as his best man. They were probably already waiting in the judge's office. Well, they would have to wait a little longer. Lana was having a wardrobe malfunction that made her feel more embarrassed than Janet Jackson at the Super Bowl.

This is what she got for choosing a beaded, long sleeved gown. When Lana and her darling fiancée decided to marry around Christmas (to take full advantage of a honeymoon in the Caribbean, of course) the bride got it in her head to commission a wintery dress that nobody would be expecting.

A Fated Night

They thought she would show up in a beaded white bikini? Well! Her reputation had begun to precede her, hadn't it? But when her mother and sister saw the unveiling of a hand stitched princess gown complete with beaded bodice and lace-laden sleeves, they were speechless. *Just what I wanted.* Lana had to admit it was a look that suited her. When the beads weren't popping off and rolling on the floor, anyway.

The seamstress yelled at her to sit still and to please put down the giant bouquet of white lilies and poinsettias because they decapitated the woman responsible for fixing Lana's dress. She couldn't help it! Lana wanted to make sure she looked absolutely perfect when she posed for pictures with her new husband. These pictures were going to be hung up in her house, sitting on her desk, and – most importantly – sent to the society papers all over the world. Lana and Ken's relationship was a point of gossip for the local scandal rags. Didn't help they were all *online* now. They would want pictures as soon as possible. Some startup called *The Daily Social* pooled together their meager resources and offered the bridal couple a sizable sum to have first dibs on their wedding photos. Lana had half a mind to buy out the company. Or at least buy the building they operated out of.

"How's my hair?" she asked her mother.

Juliet twitched to not have her champagne glass instantly refilled. *Functioning alcoholics. I swear to God...* "Lovely, as always, dear." She put down the champagne glass and occupied her hand by slamming it against her hip. Her glittery gold gown was almost the same color as the champagne she judiciously drank when she thought nobody was looking. "Suppose I'm expected to tell you what to do on your wedding night. Not that you need help with that." She scoffed. "Everyone knows it's a miracle the man is buying the cow when you gave the milk away for free for years."

Actually, it was his milk he was giving away. Lana didn't say that simply because she didn't want to make her mother vomit. Yet now that she thought about it… how much semen did a man usually ejaculate in a year? Because Lana was good enough to make her fiancé give up twice as much for free. *We've got the paparazzi photos to prove it!* Lana didn't care. Why, one would almost think *someone* had purposely sold some scandalous sex pics to a certain paper right before she was due to buy her first property on her own. Shook the buyer right in his boots to see her curvaceous body march into his office right after seeing it half naked and bobbing in her fiancé's lap. *I was meant for porn. Too bad I have success elsewhere.* The exhibitionist in her had already impressed sex clubs across the world.

"You're jealous because we're richer than the family." Lana was worth more than a few million now, even without the Losers inheritance. Ken had more, but together they were investing at a rate of return that would make them billionaires within seven years. Assuming they took care of the money and didn't blow it. Lana intended to make that money work for her. "Which you shouldn't be. You always told Inid and me to marry so rich we made your grandmother resurrect so she could have another heart attack. Well, I did my job. Go after her now." She pointed to her sister, texting on her phone.

A Fated Night

"I did tell you that, and I meant every word. Which is why you almost made me choke to see how flippant you were with an Andrews son. You should've at least locked it down with a baby by now. He can still stand you up at the altar. Least you could've done was withhold all the kinky sex until he put a ring on you."

"Or a baby in me, yes, I know." No babies for Lana so far. Probably never, if conversations with Ken leading up to this wedding were to be believed. He had plenty of brothers to keep the family going should he end up being the childless one. Suited Lana *fine*, since she never had a maternal bone in her body. (Not even for pets, if it could be believed.) She was pragmatic. Lana had no business carrying and birthing little Lanas for the sole purpose of trapping a rich man in her money-grubbing snare. Besides, she wanted to make her own money. Ken was her partner, not her meal ticket, no matter how Juliet saw her new son-in-law. "You haven't said a single thing about this white dress, though."

"Oh, please, Lana. I wasn't a virgin when I wore my white dress, either."

"Lana's like... the least virginal person in the world," Inid said.

The seamstress cleared her throat. It wasn't enough to drown out what Juliet said next. "Really, Lana, how will a man stay married to you when you're out every other weekend looking for new boyfriends?"

"I am not." Leave it to Juliet to get it all wrong. How did she find out about Ken and Lana's favorite past time? *First time we had a threesome, I knew it was true love.* There was another gorgeous woman in the bedroom and he *wasn't* obsessed with her? Only Lana? *That's when I knew I was going to marry him!* Okay, no. She knew she was going to marry him when their next threesome was with another man and Ken put his stories up for truth.

Lana got all hot and bothered thinking about it. Too bad there wasn't any point to that until this wedding was over with.

Once her dress was fixed, she had about five minutes to get her ass to the judge's chambers on time. The man was an old friend of Ken's family and had allowed the couple to tastefully decorate it to look more like a Christmastime wedding. Lana didn't care how the actual wedding looked. The biggest photo ops would be the next day when they held a reception at the country club. How many brides got to say they wore their dress more than once?

Juliet's worries were for naught. Ken's nuclear family were all in attendance. Three strapping young men stood around their brother for photos while Lana's new mother-in-law (whom she still wasn't sure she got along with) looked on with pride. The moment Ken looked over and saw his bride, his businesslike smile disappeared in favor of one filled with the kind of romantic love that used to make Lana want to throw up.

She still wanted to throw up. The nerves had finally punched her in the stomach.

***

A Fated Night

"Of course," someone muttered. "Take your time."

"Don't take pictures of that!" Ken's mother scolded one of her younger sons. "Really, what kind of family are they making us out to be?"

They can criticize me all they want, but it's my damned wedding and I'll kiss my bride for however long I want. Everyone swooned and clapped when Ken dipped Lana over his leg and kissed her the moment they signed the marriage license. So maybe some tongue slipped in there. And, uh, maybe Lana slapped his ass even though both of their families watched on. Ken was too happy to give a shit about his family judging him.

The only thing that could break them up prematurely was Lana's cell phone going off in her sister's purse. Inid popped it open and withdrew the phone while watching her sister make out with her new husband. Lana patted Ken's shoulder, telling him to let her up and give her some air.

My pleasure. Lana was soon out of his grasp and answering her phone. She would only do that if it was something so important that she would interrupt her own wedding for it.

"Yes?" she answered, spellbinding her husband in her radiant gown and with those full red lips. "Make it quick. I just got married."

The room was awkwardly quiet. What *was* the protocol for a bride taking a call at her wedding ceremony? Should they scold her?

Lana's eyes grew so large that her curled lashes almost disappeared into her forehead. "What! Today? Are you kidding me?" She lowered her phone and addressed Ken a few feet away. "It's the lawyer. The sellers want to do it *today* or not at all!"

"What?" Ken almost didn't believe her. They were in the process of purchasing one of the most lucrative office buildings in the city, but the seller was waffling and told them they would reconvene once the couple was back from their honeymoon. "You've got to be kidding."

Lana was back on the phone. "Oh my God, if we don't go there and sign the papers right now, we don't get it at all!"

Half the room sighed in resignation. Their plays as a power couple were already so well known that neither the Andrews nor the Losers could be surprised that this was transpiring on a wedding day. All they could do was follow them out of the City Hall and to the limo waiting for them on the street. Rain threatened to fall. The sun was already hidden behind the skyline, and the day was so dark this late in the year that Lana shone like a white and gold beacon that turned more than a few heads.

Their families waved at them as the limo drove off, Lana still glued to her phone and fighting with her large diamond earrings as they continued to tangle in her hair. Ken attempted to fix them for her, but Lana was so wound up that *he* almost ended up on the other side of her ire – and that was a place he never, ever wanted to be.

"Bunny," he cooed, trying to take the phone away from her. "Let me handle this. We'll head back home, change, and then go down to his office…"

A Fated Night

"Oh, hell no!" Lana batted his hand away. "We're going down there dressed like this! He'll see how much I want that fucking piece of trash-glass when he sees me showing up in a wedding dress!"

"I don't doubt that." But did it mean Ken had to sign over millions of dollars in a tuxedo? Apparently. Man, if the press wanted a helluva photo of their wedding day? They were about to get it.

"No, you don't tell him that Lana Losers is on her way there," she spat into her phone, cheeks as red as her lips, "you tell him Lana *Andrews* is on her way!"

While Lana yelled at their real estate lawyer on the phone, Ken leaned over and lightly kissed her throat. His fingers felt a bump beneath the collar of her dress. Further inspection revealed the little brass bunny he bought her when they first met.

"Mmf!" Lana almost dropped her phone when her husband sideswiped her with a kiss to rival the one back at City Hall. *I can't help it. She's so hot when she's being both romantic and Queen of the Real Estate World at the same time.* He had to have her.

Now.

"We'll call you when we get there," he said into the phone he stole. Ken snapped it shut, told the driver upfront to do some circles around the block, and resumed kissing his naughty bride. But not before gathering her dress into his hands and fishing for the garter he really, really hoped she was wearing.

"Seriously?" she said between kisses. "Right now? We're gonna consummate this thing right now?"

"We sure are, Mrs. Andrews." He had her cornered, hand stroking her thigh and mouth pressing through the beaded lace of her bodice. "You wanna pull a power play and intimidate the man into selling his building to us? Make sure he knew we fucked on the way here."

A bit over the top, sure, but Ken figured that was going to become their trademark in the many, many years of wedded bliss to come. It must've been fate he met a woman so compatible with his sexual urges and thirst for world domination.

Yes. Fate. Something like what he had with Lana was never left up to mere, fallible chance.

A Fated Night

Cynthia Dane spends most of her time writing in the great Pacific Northwest. And when she's not writing, she's dreaming up her next big plot and meeting all sorts of new characters in her head.

She loves stories that are sexy, fun, and cut right to the chase. You can always count on explosive romances - both in and out of the bedroom - when you read a Cynthia Dane story.

Falling in love. Making love. Love in all shades and shapes and sizes. Cynthia loves it all!

Connect with Cynthia on any of the following:

Website: http://www.cynthiadane.com
Twitter: http://twitter.com/cynthia_dane
Facebook: http://facebook.com/authorcynthiadane

Printed in Great Britain
by Amazon